LOVE ON TRIAL

The **Scylla and Charybdis of Love Relationships**

Hector Warnes

Pen Press Publishers
London

LOVE ON TRIAL

The **Scylla and Charybdis of Love Relationships**

Hector Warnes

First published in Great Britain by
Pen Press Publishers Limited
39-41 North Road
Islington
London N7 9DP

ISBN 1 900796 61 9

A catalogue record for this book is available
from the British Library

Cover design by Bridget Tyldsley from
Rubens, *Allegory of Peace and War*, National Gallery

Contents

Preface

"Ein Zeichen sind wir, deutunglos
Schmerzlos sind wir und haben fast
Die Sprache in der Fremde verloren"
(Hoelderlin's Mnemosyne).

This is a story of an intense, stormy and tragic love relationship that, like a ship lost at sea, was wrecked against the rocks of reality. It could be considered as a paradigm of male-female divisions, repeating the archetypical couple's conflicts from the beginning of time such as Adam and Eve in the Judeo-Christian tradition; Kayomorts and Gachorum in the Persian tradition; Prasrimpo and Prasrinmo in the Chinese tradition; Aske and Embla in the Scandinavian tradition; Parucha and Vigadj in the Hindu tradition and Adima and Adimi in the tradition of Hindustan. It could also be regarded as an externalized conflict, originating from the unconscious male or female (androgynous) counterpart, mirroring each other in a dangerous game (the Jungian animus or anima).

Vincent was an indefatigable traveller who found the world his natural habitat and explored, like a medieval scholar, all areas of knowledge and experience. Moirae, on the contrary, valued security above everything else and took a dim view of any adventurous undertaking. For many years both were deeply in love with each other, had several children and were heavily committed to their professional endeavour. The poems written by Vincent are largely autobiographical in the sense of an interplay between reality and fiction. In some instances the very subject (sub-jectum, subjection, subjugate, en-thral, dominate) is found slipping away or sliding off a signifier to represent another signifier for another subject in another scene.

The poems are very sensual, in the sense of epidermic, possessing an unsettling and lamenting intonation which is conveyed by words in pursuit of its own meaning. We find images that combine, in many guises, the pathos and timelessness of love, blending traumas since the dawn of history ('the horror of history') that parallel their own mishaps, downfalls, repetitions and separations. The poems are built upon an endless invocation of symbolic deaths, rebirths, reincarnations, ritual sacrifices, losses, bereavements, self-deception, forlornness and exile.

In their mid-lives the couple endured a deadly blow brought about by adversity (Lat. ad-verto, turned against or adversary), due largely to Vincent's failures, which shook the very foundations of their beings and   fractured their lives like a crystal following the lines of its faults. Ever since that shattering event a shadow was cast over their future and over the very fabric of their closeness. The sense of safety and impregnability that formerly characterized their relationship was undermined, nothing could be taken for granted any longer. The world for both became inauspicious, ill-omened and uncertain. For both... until she decided to throw overboard ballast and found a safe haven where to anchor even if it meant the end of her relationship with Vincent which was, by then, depleting and thwarting her vitality. The wooing letters, some sentimental other conceptual, written by Vincent to Moirae left her unmoved and unfeeling. She would display a dauntless aloofness, a secretive and cryptic demeanour that would fire Vincent's imagination. Consistently, she would shun any dialogue or interaction that could appease, counter or neutralize his feverish state of mind. There were, however, occasional nonverbal cues and unintentional responses that nurtured his hope for a reunion.

This is the story of an idyllic relationship that came to grief and floundered against all odds. It could have been felt or written by anybody, at any time, anywhere, under any condition or social status. Couples who experience a similar breakdown in their relationship are often able to trace the cause or causes of the journey's end with the 'Lebensgefaehrte' (companion for life) and 'Leidensgefaehrte' (companion in suffering or trouble). There are, on the other hand, many other factors that may elude their search and that are adumbrated in the correspondence between Vincent and Moirae. Unsolved grievances with parental figures are paramount. The letters show human non-fulfilment, subjugation, erring, dereliction and imperfections:..."que notre volonté était née aveugle; que ses désirs étaient aveugles, sa conduite encore plus aveugle, et qu'il ne fallait pas s'étonner si, parmi tant d'aveuglement, l'homme etait dans un égarement continuel?" (*p.194: La Rochefoucauld - Maximes et Reflexions - Editions Gallimard, Paris, 1965*).

Vincent had a consuming passion (in the sense of inclination, 'ivresse d'amour', ardor, longing, cupidity, allurement and 'Leidenschaft') for Moirae, a passion which was carved purely and empirically (Gr. pure, pyros or pyr and en, in the pyros, fire) resulting in a state of unrequited love. A Greek goddess, Ate, was the embodiment of those forces associated with blind passion such as infatuation (a gullible and unsuspecting state), moral dim-sightedness, woe, outrage and madness. He did not, however, succumb to despair, that old familiar despair that made him look into the abyss while feeling the irresistible lure of its gaping and staring void. Eventually, he was able to crawl out of darkness, that darkness that clouded his vision and led him astray. He was also able to limit the scope of her grip on him. She was no longer seen at every turn of the road, felt in every filament of his being, evoked with every hint of suggestion that vaguely had some associations with her and finally, she would not longer visit him in every dream. Neither poetry, philosophy nor psychoanalysis could describe adequately the agonies of love lost and the flashes of creativity that restored Vincent to sanity. When he drifted apart into a solitary and insular exile the 'mystique' of his love for Moirae was his single guiding, redeeming and live-saving star. The Latin word 'solus' (Gr.'holos', whole) is at the root of the words solitary and solid. Vincent found wholeness in aloneness. His ability to tolerate utter loneliness, to work through his grief by writing about the ill-fated relationship and his striving not to proscribe his loving and hopeful feelings into sheer oblivion or facile substitutions proved to be his salvation.

Hector Warnes

Introduction

'Le coeur a ses raisons que la raison ne connaît point.' (The heart has its reasons which the mind knows nothing of). Blaise Pascal, *Pensées:* 4-277.

With each separation his love for her grew stronger while her love for him withered.

In Greek and Celtic Mythology there are metaphors that convey the central dynamics of love, namely, fusion versus separateness, likeness versus difference and love versus hatred. Psyche loved Eros during the dark hours of the night. One night driven by curiosity she discovered his real identity which caused him to fly away. She did not spare any means to find him, even travelling to the underworld. After many tribulations they were reunited. In this myth we elicit a conflict between knowledge and feelings and the many trials that true love has to encounter. Oisin was stirred by homesickness for the mortal world and Niamh, tired of his laments, allowed him to fly to Earth on a magic horse from which he accidentally fell to the ground. Once he landed on Earth he aged considerably and languished for Niamh's embraces in his last moments. Oisin's nostalgia brought an end to a blissful union.

Circe, a witch, was notorious for turning Odysseus's men into swines. She was also able to charm Odysseus himself and fathered him two sons. In interpersonal dynamics this process of induction and attributions may cause the other to believe he is actually bad or to fall into an unanticipated spell.

In Greek mythology the sirens were servants of Persephone, the death queen, who ordered them to bring souls to her. The sirens were enchantresses because they could seduce and cast spells. As in Goya's series *'The dream of reason produce monsters'* many nightmares of an individual may be transformed into collective myths and many severe privations are turned into chimeras. At the height of fervour and adoration reason is often asleep and misery, sadness, anger, despair and acts of revenge may take hold of a person when that ideal vacillates. But, nevertheless, an invisible bond, a subtle thought with sensibility, an affinity beyond words and an exquisite receptivity is evoked by a simple gesture of gaze of the loved one.

Elizabeth Barrett Browning noted the exhilaration arising from being in love:

> *"The face of all the world is changed, I think,*
> *Since first I heard the foot steps of thy soul*
> *Move still, oh, still, beside me, as they stole*
> *Betwixt me and the dreadful outer brink*
> *Of obvious death, where I who thought to sink*
> *Was caught up into love and taught the whole*
> *Of life in a new rhythm..."* (p.9)

> *"How do I love thee? Let me count the ways.*
> *I love thee to the depth and breadth and height*
> *My soul can reach, when feeling out of sight*
> *For the ends of Being and Ideal Grace."* (p.35)

2

Passionate love is a shared fantasy, a longing for fusion, an over valuation or idealization of another person who may not live up to that projective image, a tyranny of possessiveness and jealousy, an interplay of sameness and difference, a terror of loss and separation, a neediness that requires a nurturing other and an inflation of subjectivity that at times blurs the sense of reality. In the extreme cases love can be lustful, devouring, dependent, demanding, exacting or an act of oblation, an offering of oneself not based on lack but on a surplus of generosity and acceptance.

St.Augustine described love for that elusive Deus absconditus very much like human love. In his *Confessions* he wrote:

'Late have I loved you, beauty so old and so new: late have I loved you. And see, you were within and I was in the external world and sought you there, and in my unlovely state I plunged into those lovely created things which you made. You were with me, and I was not with you. The lovely things kept me far from you, though if they did not have their existence in you, they had no existence at all. You called and cried out loud and shattered my deafness. You were radiant and resplendent, you put to flight my blindness. You were fragrant, and I drew in my breath and now pant after you. I tasted you, and I feel but hunger and thirst for you. You touched me, and I am set on fire to attain the peace which is yours...' (p.201, *Confessions* - Translated by Henry Chadwick - Oxford University Press, 1991).

Love may lead to mortification or self-flagellation and, paradoxically, may re-enact the via cruces of Jesus, the Golgota, that each man harbours within himself. Man may even, out of all proportion, find God and or love in the affirmation of ugliness, shame, misery, infamy or illness. The mortification of the flesh is invariably a desire to overcome a haunting sensuality or a guilty resentment that is associated

3

with the fall of man. For the Zen Buddhist practitioner asceticism is not, like for the Christian, the affirmation of guilt, suffering and expiation but a way to overcome suffering, to flee from hedonism, to liberate the mind from earthly chains, and to develop a higher state of consciousness.

Love is thus plagued with unexpected aberrations, deflections and disappointments. A change of fortune, an unwilling separation, a will to live out fully an inner script, the passage of time, a collusive self-defeating interaction but principally one's own compulsion to repeat and act out unconscious conflicts are some of the factors that weaken or devitalize it.

In a remarkable poem-song *'Ne me quitte pas'* Jacques Brel despairs over being abandoned. In the first part he invokes Lethe or oblivion of the past, of misunderstandings or hurts. In the second part the lover offers love beyond time and death, promises 'pearls of rain' and a kingdom of love where she would be the queen. In the third part the lover tells her stories in an effort to postpone the fatal outcome by creativity. In the fourth part he still hopes that her love for him would one day be rekindled. In the fifth part he sinks in silence, ceases to cry and simply observes her surreptitiously with his hungry eyes. Finally, in a storm of despair, he begs her to let him become the shadow of her shadow, the shadow of her hands, the shadow of her dog and with each strophe he repeats: please, don't leave me, don't leave me, don't leave me, don't leave me.

Ne me quitte pas

'Ne me quitte pas
Il faut oublier
Tout peut s'oublier
Qui s'enfuit déjà
Oublier le temps
Des malentendus
Et le temps perdu
A savoir comment
Oublier ces heures
Qui tuaient parfois
A coups du pourquoi
Le coeur du bonheur
Ne me quitte pas
Ne me quitte pas
Ne me quitte pas
Ne me quitte pas

Moi je t'offrirai
Des perles de pluie
Venues de pays
Où il ne pleut pas
Je creuserai la terre
Jusqu'après ma mort
Pour couvrir ton corps
D'or et de lumière
Je ferai un domaine
Où l'amour sera roi
Où l'amour sera loi
Où tu seras reine
Ne me quitte pas
Ne me quitte pas

Ne me quitte pas
Ne me quitte pas.

Ne me quitte pas
Je t'inventerai
Des mots insensés
Que tu comprendras
Je te parlerai
De ces amants là
Qui ont vu deux fois
Leurs coeurs s'embraser
Je te raconterai
L'histoire de ce roi
Mort de n'avoir pas
Pu te rencontrer
Ne me quitte pas
Ne me quitte pas
Ne me quitte pas
Ne me quitte pas.

On a vu souvent
Rejaillir le feu
D'un ancien volcan
Qu'on croyait trop vieux
Il es paraît-il
Des terres brûlées
Donnant plus de blé
Qu'un meilleur avril
Et quand vient le soir
Pour qu'un ciel flamboie
Le rouge et le noir
Ne s'épousent-ils pas
Ne me quitte pas

Ne me quitte pas
Ne me quitte pas
Ne me quitte pas

Ne me quitte pas
Je ne vais plus pleurer
Je ne vais plus parler
Je me cacherai là
A te regarder
Danser et sourire
Et à t'écouter
Chanter et puis rire
Laisse-moi devenir
L'ombre de ton ombre
L'ombre de ta main
L'ombre de ton chien
Ne me quitte pas
Ne me quitte pas
Ne me quitte pas
Ne me quitte pas'

(pp.167-169 - Jacques Brel, *Oeuvre Integrale*, Editions Robert Lafont, Paris, 1982).

Correspondence

This book is the narrative of the ebb and flow of love between Moirae and Vincent during their eighteen years relationship based on a profusion of letters and the musings of the author. The language of love is underscored while the more historical or mundane aspects of the relationship are omitted.

There are many aspects in this intense love relationship that can be readily identified. Attractiveness, infatuation, offering, merging vs separation, conflicts (e.g. trust vs mistrust, dependence vs independence, love vs aggression), privation, disappointments, adversity, loss and grief, invocation, thralldom, supplication and glimpses of regeneration. Some of these latter phases become clearer as Moirae was unable to withstand the catastrophic events in their lives which led to more separations. She gradually withdrew her love for Vincent who remained utterly enthralled and kept on writing her wooing letters which were not reciprocated.

"My love for you has crystalized throughout the ages and has gained the strength of a diamond. What madness to leave you. I have the illusion of seeing you everywhere as if your shadow has fallen upon my soul. Entering your realm is frought with dangers. Would I be strong, virile, without blemish? Would I break taboos? Would I fulfil your dreams? Would you accept me with all my insecurities and love me for ever? Or would you be like a Druid priestess urge this poor mortal to pass through ritual sacrifice? All my being is taken up by your being. I see through you - I taste through you. Your eyes give me a sense of the infinite. I am tossed about from doubt, to despair, to loving, sensing and grieving your absence. Please tell me I am not a worm eating away your beautiful soul. I am dying to hold you again in my arms. Our love pact reassures me and makes me less fearful of my own empty spaces.

'The woods are lovely, dark and deep,
But I have promises to keep,
And miles to go before I sleep,
And miles to go before I sleep.' (R. Frost)

With all consuming love,

Vincent"

"I never want to feel a distance between us. You are so special to me - you have become part of me and I will carry you always in my dreams. I feel we could truly love and transcend the constraints and conventions of this world. Your love for me has made me whole again. Sometimes I fear it matters little who I am as long as I am strong and independent - strong enough to shoulder the responsibility and protect you from my weaknesses.

You ask how come I cannot harbour your image in the sanctuary of my heart - that I need your presence to rekindle that flame. All I know is that your image is not enough - without you I am lonely and inconsolable - with you I am

9

joyful and alive. Oh dearest - we'll get through this difficult painful time but see no virtue or gain in it of the emotional kind.

Your willing prisoner,

Moirae"

"Sorry to hear that you were so much affected by our separation. I felt as if I was tearing off a flower. I myself have been taciturn - not finding a good reason to live except in the glow of your presence and the beat of your heart. How many times must we part before your are convinced of my love for you. How many times must we die before our love becomes the eternal reflection of a universal music. You are my only dream. Not capturing it might endanger my very life. A primitive force has been unleashed in me and chasing my soul in you has become my leitmotiv. My adoration for you requires an altar of love. Only you can unbind this wretched Prometheus from his chains. We must avoid any condition that imperils our relationship. After all we humans are like passengers of a sinking ship but loving you is like riding high on the sky - I dread the fall.

I worry about you getting cold, not eating properly, not being comforted, fretting about our reunion, languishing with aches and pangs. As for me I am more the solitary and independent kind who will die without even noticing, who will imagine that illusion, who will pine for your return and in desiring it will be transported to heights of pleasure. Departing must be our trial of fire, a sign of the tenacity of our feelings, of our capacity for endurance and the workings of our pact of blood. I dread to think that a sinister part of myself, an evil star or a thorn in my flesh will conspire to undermine the most precious gift of life: yourself. You are a part of my life, torn away by the violence of social circumstances and yet living, palpitating and yearning to be where it belongs. Time is passing, my life without you is fading and my desire for you is consuming my soul and withering my flesh.

With unrelenting love,

Vincent"

"I need you desperately - I could not survive without you. When I read your letters and you say wonderful things to me I feel myself blushing all over. What is all this in our last conversation about you being an obscure and doomed Professor like in the film *'The Blue Angel'*. I am not that much younger than you - and you certainly are nothing like that poor Professor in the film. Besides I am your steadfast devoted lover, friend, wife - everything you want me to be for ever. My darling I am so happy to have you all to myself and I am so anxious to rejoin you - I just want to close my eyes and sink into your arms - Never, never, never again we'll inflict separation on us. It is just not worth the suffering - I'll never agree to it. I long to snuggle up beside you and feel you kiss and hold me. I miss you terribly. I love you so much and I am fretting as usual about you starving to death. I want you to kiss me and tell me you will forgive my cruelty and I want to kiss all your wounds and tell you I'll forgive all your cruelties. I have lovely day dreams that we are making love. Maybe you will punish me - ravish me - take your revenge.
I am longing for you. Thousand kisses,

Moirae"

"I had a dream that I could not find you - we kept by-passing each other and I kept retracing my steps looking for you. At the end I had to answer to a tribunal about my motives. Please, don't let me challenge the Fates. My father's death, my friend's death and our separation are all a pale shadowy reflection announcing the unspeakable, unnameable certainty of the ultimate separation - death. Don't tell me that I am doomed to act out some obscure Karma of my own, to test the strength of our love under harsh circumstances, to submit to expiation for only God knows what crimes or to be transfixed in a fit of self-purification in order to attain a higher state of consciousness?

We must endeavour to navigate together to the end of times. To lose myself in the immensity of you, to adore you is my unshakable desire and my cherished ideal. There are many forms of dying but one of them is not having you within reach. Guess who is bemoaning his unfortunate fate of being set apart from the loveliest maid. The transitoriness of all things frightens me. The only certainty is my love for you - it has become ageless, timeless. I never felt so strongly for anybody. My love for you has brought a transformation in me that cut across personal ambitions, materialistic goals and the mechanization of life. I am terrified of losing you. I read the stars and wait for that propitious moment - Kairos - in order to throw myself into your being without reservations.

I am afraid about your mother's subjugation to your father, the concealment of her true feelings, and her self-abnegation for her daughters. I am afraid about your father's infidelities, overbearing dominance, his rancour and his iron rule.

Identifications, counter-identifications, vulnerabilities and fantasies may be re-enacted in spite of oneself. Every victim scans the world for a victimizer. Are we going to endure all the tribulations and tests of love and come out victorious and unscarred? Your love is the keystone of my life not unlike for the gambler who plays 'Russian roulette' with fate. We should not fall in the trap of self-complacency nor in the trap of debasing the other person's needs. No one who feels inadequate or lacks self-esteem should bolster his ego by degrading his partner nor should he out of jealousy or envy lose his sense of reality and fairness or try to impose on the other unattainable expectations.

A partner may be tempted to facilitate or to inhibit these urges. You are my complement, an extension of my self, my soother and my oasis.

The last time I hung up the phone I felt in a state of frantic aloneness. The night grew awesome in its nakedness. The streets were cold and deserted. Time began dilating and spreading its threatening tentacles and I stood feeling utterly lost. I realized that exile, the homeless malady, was spitting me in the face and my unswerving love for you increased that vulnerability like a gaping wound. I am not a fighter, I am just a dreamer, of dreams that slip through my fingers and remain remote. Your nectar is my only remedy to life sickness.

I can't think of any more sweet and desirable than being with you,

Vincent"

"The thought of actually setting up a home with you sends me into rapturous anticipation. I am feeling so broody. Nest building seems the most delightful occupation. Spending the rest of my life with you illuminates the future. I want to experience the feeling when I do arrive that it is the last journey - that from now on we will be bound together for ever. How can I measure up to your letters? They are so ardent and passionate. When I read them I want you there to respond with all my heart. I am feeling so amorous. I am thinking of your body - your warmth, your kisses, your eyes... Will you hear all my unspoken longings?

We are embarking on such an uncertain mission - with so many dangers. You are my dream and I want to grasp you and never let go. I want to put my arms around you now and cry and cry. You beg me to allow you to get a 'second wind' before you do what needs to be done for our relationship. I love every aspect of you even your weaknesses. I love your complicated emotional passions. I love your many strengths, your talent in your work, your altruism, your poetic dreamy side, your responsible attitude, I desire you more than ever. Please don't let anger, hurt feelings come between us. I am terribly sorry for the times I have hurt your feelings - inadverently or deliberately - forgive me. I don't want to cause you pain and if I do I want to salve it. I long for the same response from you - salve for my hurt feelings. Lay aside your pride and hear me because I truly love you. You are my most precious treasure, my secret delight, my answer to a maidens' prayer...

Infinite kisses,

Moirae"

"I am sorry for having shown my darker side, my ambivalence, my exasperation but it takes two persons to escalate a conflict and I often hear how much of a victim you are and how much of a villain I am. Your bitterness is bottomless and your desire to find faults is relentless. Are you my Nemesis? It is ironic: my love for you has been growing while your love for me have been shrinking. I seem

14

to have less and less to reproach you for while you have a sustained ability to accumulate grudges and recriminations. This in no way means that you do not have some valid points. You give me an ultimatum and make me feel like a little boy whose bossy nanny shakes her finger at. I am ready to make any sacrifices for our relationship. I give you carte blanche to abuse me but keep on loving me. Please disregard anything I wrote, I said or I did but do not disregard my intense closeness and love for you. Why can we not mitigate our aches? You were magnificent during the turbulent times. I just want you to know that my love for you has never been in question.

How can I fulfil all your heart's desires in this imperfect and wretched world? Perhaps, I have been for far too long outwitting the fairies, befriending the furies but I have been made captive by you, my incomparable sorceress.

Soon we shall be together. You will be walking towards me, posing your evanescent gaze, your ethereal mind on my no less melting state of being. My life is guided by milestones, but lighthouses which always point to you or to representations of you.

Your life and mine are intertwined for ever regardless,

Vincent"

"When we do finally get together I will rediscover all the desire that seems to have died inside me since you left. I need you there - when we are apart I am not fully alive. I hope you are no longer jealous and doubting my faithfulness. I may have given you cause by my flirtatious manner which after all springs from my identification with my father's egotism and my mother's insecurity. I have to work hard on not identifying with mother - as her behaviour is totally inappropriate for me and my situation. This is why it upsets you so much - and probably explains why I have stimulated your jealousy. Really you are crazy to torture yourself. I think you are the only person for me. I am so obsessed with your image - other people barely impinge on my awareness. We must never part again even if we have to chain ourselves together. Oh dearest creature I am lost between madness and sanity, certainty and doubt. The only unchanging centre is you and my everlasting love. You always find delightful new ways of telling me how much you love me. I miss you. I can't wait to be with you. I can't tell you how much I long to be in your comforting arms. When I see you again I am going to need a terrible amount of cuddling to make up for this barren worrying time - I am sure you feel the same. It will be so fantastic to rejoin you. That is the thought that sustains me - it can't be too soon. I am constantly sending all sorts of hungry longing, lonely, loving messages to you - every minute of the day. I am languishing with this aching need and that will go on until you hold me close in your arms and we are permanently reunited. How can I hurry up the time. I feel like going into hibernation so I could sleep through it and wake up to find myself with you.

I adore you - a hundred million kisses,

Moirae"

"You are foremost in my mind, I cherish every moment we spent together, I like to be with you, inside you, besides you, on you, behind you, in the most recondite parts of your being... You must keep me inside you, locked in your heart forever, whether I am with you or not - would you promise me? It is a source of endless pleasure to imagine you walking towards me, with your radiant smile and that special gravitational pull.

Your presence will be my panacea, will undo all wrongs and will repair any damage. I am so desperate to have you in my arms, to caress you and to tell you, looking deep into your eyes, ivre d'amour, how much you mean to me.

Please, forgive my flaws. I know that I am caught up in the dialectics of being a hero, an antihero, an imposter and the need to invent a hero in my unheroic conduct. I dreamed that I was rushing to meet you when I was assailed by two huge tigers. In order to avoid an attack I played possum on my back and one of the tigers took a bite at my foot. When you turned back to call for help the tiger released its bite and let me go. I guess, I feel threatened by our increasing closeness. I am jealous of your fantasies, of the people you talk to, you look at or you look into... jealous of your youth, your past and your future; of your naturalness, your passion, your desires; jealous of myself, of your thirst for life and your responsive palpitating body; jealous of intrusions, perturbations, detours, innuendos and shadows. The sea is stormy and the sky is overcast, a roaring tempest is gathering momentum. You are my compass, my lighthouse and my star. You are my lifeline, you are vital like air to me, you are my spiritual sustenance, without you I would fade away and wither.

Gottfried Keller in *Der Gruene Heinrich* wrote:

'I hope my dear Lee, that you may never learn from your own personal experience the peculiar and piquant truth of the plight of Odysseus when he appeared naked and covered with mad before the eyes of Nausicaa and her maidens. Shall I tell you how that can happen? Let us look into our example. If you are wandering about in a foreign land, far from your home and from all that hold dear, if you have seen and heard many things, have known sorrow and care, and are wretched and forlorn, then without fail you will dream one night that you

are coming near to your home; you will see its gleaning and
shining in the fairest colours, and the sweetest, dearest and
most beloved forms will move towards you. Then suddenly
you will become aware, that you are in rags, naked and dusty.
You will be seized with a nameless shame and dread, you will
seek to find covering and to hide yourself and you will awake
bathed in sweat. This, so long as men breathe, is the dream of
the unhappy wanderer.'

Without you I feel like a stranger to myself - walking on a tight rope and wondering whether it would be preferable to fall. I see your hand reaching out at the other side of the abyss, encouraging me to bridge the gap that separates us. For some reasons you are so much better than me at heights. I am so eager to see my better half since I am in a state of incompleteness without you. You have the most engaging and tender personality I ever met: dreamy eyes, an accepting smile, passion, fervour and poise. Your letters are intoxicating and delightful and I could go on raving about you.

With incredible, ever growing love and devotion,

Vincent"

"I don't know how to wipe out your doubts. I had liberated ideas and an oversized oedipal complex to contend with; I burdened you with a past you find unpalatable and which threaten to drive you away from me. It was inevitable that my first lover was an older man who did not satisfy me physically because I wasn't fit for a mature sexual relationship. He didn't satisfy me emotionally because he was not capable of really loving anyone: all he really succeeded in doing was haunting me with unfullfilment. Time has shown me that no matter how much I thought I loved him he did not go right through to the heart of me. Although I protested bitterly about my lack of sexual response I see that it was the better part of myself that was saying no. For five years I was struggling unsuccessfully to untangle myself. I sought emotional support in exchange for physical compliance - like a whore - and did not find fulfilment: I tried to be liberated and self seeking - and did not find fulfilment. Despite the fact that I accommodated strangers they never gained access to the sanctuary I reserve exclusively for you. I choose to respond to you because you are very special to me. No one ever made it with me - until I met you. You love me better than anyone and I have learnt to trust you enough to be myself. I am your treasure and your joy - Maybe I can also be your torturer - just as you can torture me - but you have to take the good with the bad: For better and for worse - till death do us part. Don't be such a perfectionist. You love me and I love you. I know you put me on a pedestal. Sweetheart, your failings of character, hurt me just as much as my failings hurt you. I don't constantly subject you to cross questioning - I make no demands as to how you spend your time. I trust you. I am closing my eyes and taking one big step over the unknown - into your arms - I am with you for life. I think I have enough strength and determination for both of us. I am not letting you throw me away. I'd rather die... I know I am safe in your heart. I know you are thinking of me at this very moment - but I long to be in your arms - you would kiss away all the self pitying tears. I don't see your departure as a desertion. We both agreed that in the present circumstances you have no alternative. Your jealousy awakes two responses in me: One is exhilaration that you care so much to make such demand - I long to be possessed exclusively by you; the second is sorrow that your jealousy grows in proportion to your love. I love you. I tremble with desire when you touch me with love or look into my eyes: I have never known such consuming love. I will never experience it with anyone else. I don't want to. I wouldn't be able to. Forgive me if I was out of time with you. I have said the wrong things at the wrong time. Thinking of how much we love each other will make me feel strong and happy, I also love being dependent on you. Do you love me more than ever? We have to make up for lost time when we are together again. When you hold me close in your arms I feel peace and security. When we make love I feel we are immersed in a sort of boundless sea.

Your own true,

Moirae"

"Your last three letters, Shakespeare's sonnets and your card made me so happy, dissipated all doubts and brought freshness and light into my heart. You have a wonderful combination of common sense and intuition. You are also honest, warm, full of wit and spontaneity. Your letters help me to sort out the unreal from the real, transform the aridity of my heart and clear away the burden of my grief. My love for you has become a certainty and a religion. Life without you would be worthless. The thought of holding your hands for ever makes me soar in the skies. John Keats expressed the way I feel about you: *'The more I have known you, the more I have loved you in every way - even my jealousies have been agonies of love; in the hottest fit I ever had I would have died for you... You are always new. The last of your kisses was ever the sweetest; the last smile the brightest; the last movement the gracefulest...'* or John Donne's felicitous phrase: *'Twice or thrice had I love thee before I knew thy face or name'*. You are creative, tender and determined which is a bliss to overcome any obstacles. Your last words are still ringing in my ears: 'let us be brave'; your last look is still burning my soul. Mourning for my father has been replaced by a languid, sweet, arcane and eternal dream - you. I dreamed that I was holding my father's hands which were pale and cold, telling him of my homecoming to take care of him. I woke up weeping and thinking how much I loved my father as a child. I am totally committed to you. No other woman can make me reach the heights you can. I can no longer bear the cold, bare and silent space that signifies your absence. I did not think it was possible to combine companionship, sensuality, intellectual challenge and love, all in one relationship. Would you help me overcome the only motive of discord, my jealousy? No matter whether it is based on real flirtatiousness, innuendos, fantasized or anticipated rivalry, would you dispel my doubts like I wish to erase yours?

You are the measure of all what I have and I don't have. Until I experienced this artless surrender for your love I thought that the Sorrows of Young Werther of Goethe was a leap into a romantic Todeslieb. Now I understand it fully. Please, give me the strength to bear this separation. I seem to be under the spell of a Pagan goddess. I live from phone call to phone call, from letter to letter. Everything in-between is loneliness and despair. It is sheer existence. You bring completeness into my being, lucidity and harmony. Your voice brings a halo to things, a warmth to my feelings and a yearning to reach out for your hand. I understand the mystic who feels that he is only a fragment of the universe consumed by an everlasting passion for God.

With fathomless love,

Vincent"

"I adore you - talking to you is heaven. I feel completely secure in your love. You must feel the same in mine. I know our relationship is made to last and get better and better despite the ups and downs. I love you desperately, I miss you terribly and on top of all the other problems I worry how you are getting on in such a lonely hostile environment. I am longing to be with you and wishing we had not inflicted this separation on ourselves. We are such a pair of idiots - we always seem to make the wrong decisions. You know that you are my only desire - you always will be. Without you I am going around in a haze, thinking of you all the time: waking, sleeping...

What is all this about the flaws behind you self-deception. Don't be so hard on yourself. I feel supremely confident that our love relationship will survive any test. You on the other hand, being of a more pessimistic bent of mind allow yourself to be tortured by the fear of what you fear most. I love you so much, I admire you and I believe you have all the qualities we need to harmonize together. Time will be our friend and not our enemy. You will see that I am right when we look back over our past. You have become the source of all joy for me. You are everything to me. I marvel at you - everything about you delights me - I treasure your ability to help me, your patience, your sense of humour and your tenderness. Oh, how I wish I never left you. Your wonderful letters set me yearning to hold you tight and never to let go. My body feels neglected and I am longing for your touch that makes me whole and happy. I am totally wound up in you. My life has taken a dream like quality with undercurrents of you which surface at night. I will give up all my past and present to be with you if that is what is necessary. I am determined to spend my life with you.

My love forever,

Moirae"

"Looking at the ivy-covered crumbling walls, wild roses, willows trailing their branches into the water I am thinking of you...

'Ah no. If vivid dreams at night,
If keen remembrances by day,
Can fetter Time's untiring flight,
Those moments are not passed away.' (Gerald Griffin).

Do you still love me with that gnawing intensity?

I am thinking of the picture of Icarus and Dedalus fleeing from the infamous labyrinth where they were imprisoned by the Minotaurus. Icarus' fall was attributed to his keen ambition and pride. Why his fall was not regarded as one of the great tragedies? The agonies of every man affects me deeply. I seem to be more caught in the pathos than in the ethos of life. This very pathos has opened up my heart to injuries, equivocations, and to intimations of dangers that lie ahead.

You are exquisite, delicate and loving. I know I cannot expect absolute and sacrificial love but I dread the chilling edge of unreality, the shivering encounter with death, the duplicity, falsity, betrayal and less than total commitment. Perhaps, all these tendencies are dragons that I must kill within myself before being worthy of your love. But never doubt that in spite of my imperfections my love for you is the most permanent and real thing I have ever experienced. I revere you with the tender passion born out of a middle age crises (Ger. Torschluss), out of the ashes of youthful dreams when great many expectations started to narrow down. Your presence fills me, follows me everywhere, is within and without, in every single memory, in every turn of the road. Anything related to you overshadows any other consideration. But I must navigate this storm hoping to find the light house where you will be waiting for me.

I have been consoling myself looking forward to your arrival, to set on fire the infinite love and forgiveness you stow for this woeful sinner, with the anticipation of your sensuality and the fruits of a torrid season.

One must pay a price for being unkind, for deserting a loving wife, for overcoming repressed sexuality, for tempting the Furies... We must rise above all the insinuations of gloom or doom, of tear and wear, of hardship and hard luck:

'Y aqui estoy, en pavor ante el abismo
De la grave conciencia acusadora...
Reo que tiembla enfrente de si mismo' (E. Gonzalez Martinez).

Your love, your strength and your faith have swept me away. I wish I was there to protect you from intrusive, controlling and undermining influences. How many times I have told you that you were far more poetic, creative and intuitive than I was. My soul-mate, guess who at dusk cries inconsolably for you and does not dare to admit it?

I have just finished reading *'The Fisherman And His Soul'*:
'Love is better than wisdom, and more precious than riches...
The fires cannot destroy it, nor can the waters quench it. I
called on thee at dawn, and thou did not come to my call.
The moon heard thy name, yet had thou no heed of me... and
to my own hurt had I wandered away. Yet ever did thy love
abide with me, and ever was it strong... You are my mermaid
and I gladly exchange my soul for your love hoping that the
end was my beginning. I feel as if at last my restive soul has
found a harbour. I am dreading that you might be unattainable.
When shall we looking back with relief? The day when we
shall overcome our Zweisamkeit (meeting of two solitudes)
and sail together towards the sunset of our lives.'

Your last phone call left in me the morning dew, the soft and tender tone, the invigorating and imminent promise of your arrival and much more. My feelings for you are impregnated with the nuances of a garden with a diversity of flowers and scents. I have just read that a Professor left his wife and children for a menial job in order to live modestly with his mistress, a waitress. He was disgusted with the materialistic and empty course of his life. Others, like Gaugin who left his family found greater suffering but also greater creativity. Why must one pay such a high price for a leap into the unknown, into the abyss of love or creativity? My comforting thought is to spend the remainder of my days with you.

I don't know any great love relationship that did not have to encounter chagrin and torments set up by the mocking Fates. We shall survive any test of fire: *'O Oysters,'* said the Carpenter, *'you've had a pleasant run. Shall we be trotting home again? But answer came there none - and this was scarcely odd because they'd eaten every one'* (*Alice in Wonderland*). Shall we be able to escape monsters lurking in the dark corners? I am so proud to walk you in this lone road across the forest. You are my life, my muse, my reason, my hope...

With unimaginable love,

Vincent"

"I am split totally between the internal and external existence - the internal in permanent communion with you negates and makes a mockery of the external. The three months we were together practically every moment were the happiest of my life. You are my whole life - I don't want anything else. Please be careful. With your luck and unworldliness you have to take every precaution. I wear to bed your pink top to help me feel closer to you.

How can I survive without you? I carry you around in my heart. I know you are feeling the same. The most important thing is to protect our love so it is not weakened by our separation. You answer so many needs in me and nourish so many hopes. I can't believe how lucky I am that you have decided you can not be without me. My life is empty without you. Sleep with me in your dreams. We have become one person who is split in two. We have merged so much into each other. We could never reclaim ourselves. It is too late. The only real comfort during these difficult times is to have contact with you. Your letters are beautiful and poetic and I love to read them over and over. Soon we shall be reunited - not that we ever really parted in spirit. Last night when I closed my eyes and tried to fall off to sleep you floated in as a cloud to enfold me. I often get this feeling when I close my eyes and I am convinced your warm thoughts and longings for me have taken on a tangible quality - you become my second skin to support and protect me - and the warmth I feel becomes our warmth, and I feel your body stretched up against my back and your arms around my tummy and your kisses on my neck. I just know that at that moment our minds have become one and we are not separated at all - and I fall off to sleep then - in your cocoon of love.

Do you look after yourself - please do feed yourself. I hate to think of you all skin and bones. I draw from memories of you to go on even the unhappy ones give some solace - masochistic that I am. When we are together we can make a store of new memories, kisses and caresses, promises and plans to sustain our love indefinitely. Eventually it will be so strong that nothing would shake it.

A million passionate kisses are forming in my mind and travelling to you,

Moirae"

"I am trying to find a modus vivendi in this period of change, gain, loss and retrieval. You are my gain and the retrieval of my soul. There is so much insight, responsibility and acceptance in what you say that I can only express my admiration and awe. I love you to the point of being outside myself. My boundaries can not contain the feelings you have awaken in me. Sleep and appetite are fickle companions of mine and unless you take care of me both are going to trouble me. You are so considerate, so kind and so sensitive to my moods and irrational fears:

'Thy soft heart refused to discover
The faults which so many could find;
Though thy soul with my grief was acquainted,
It shrunk not to share it with me,
And the love which my spirit had painted
It never had found but in thee.' (Byron).

After you phoned I ended up making love to you, an apparition an overwhelming, undulating, palpitating form surrounding, encompassing, encircling all my being. Your immense eyes were fixed upon me, taking me in, inviting and accepting me. I entered into the warmest recesses of your being and felt the little 'hug' giving me life and a new lease on time. In you I mirror the reflections of every moment, I see you in every event, in every person no matter how vague or minimal the trait that evokes your image might be. The contemplation of you has become the source of my greatest strength and anticipation. I would never forgive myself if, after you have given everything up for me, I would not be able to make you happy. The world is cruel for lovers but we must struggle:*'with lofty thoughts, that neither evil tongues, rash judgements not the sneers of selfish people, nor all the dreary intercourse of daily life, shall ever prevail against us, or disturb our cheerful faith that all which we behold is full of blessings...'*(Wordsworth).

27

Why you keep on asking me if I am going to fall out of love? I would never stop loving you. I see you as that divine force that allows me to be grounded and that gives meaning to my life. Since I left you I died many times, I descended into hell, I underwent an agonizing self-scrutiny... You were all the time the light house that guided me and prevented me from sinking. I must admit that I experience a fleeting resentment because of this state of bondage. I am also afraid of losing you. You have made me feel again. Before you I felt like Hamlet: *'unmoved, cold and to temptation slow'*. I have been homeless for too long and an inner voice tells me that you are my home, my habitation, my source and inspiration. Guess, who is the maid who taught me what is love, contemplation and imagination? Murmuring like a mountain spring, I do love you. I know our love nest shall not be a cage. Would you tolerate my imperfections, limitations and contradictions? Would you help me cultivate that kind of unity of sensation, feeling, intuition and thinking which you seem to possess? Our love must endure all earthly and temporal blighted hope, blows reign of terror and separations because it has the qualities of a diamond at least from my perspective. Will you accept my heartfelt sorrow for not living up to your expectations? I shall kneel at your feet to beg your forgiveness.

Without you I am hollow, I am a man of straw.

Au bout de souffle,

tendrement,

Vincent"

"I can imagine what you must have felt when I left you and I am torturing myself thinking about the monstruous cruelty I inflicted on you and beg again and again your forgiveness:

'give me a kiss before you leave me, give me your lips for a moment and my imagination will make that moment live for ever.'

Vincent"

"I lost count of the times we took leave from each other. Please, forgive me for having put you through so much strain. I experienced our farewell like a sting of death, like being thrown in an empty and dark world and like walking alone in an uncertain and eerie road. However, I never seem to give up hope. I keep on waiting for that magic word of yours, for an inviting sign, for a forgiving gesture. I keep on imagining and sensing that you are my lost continent and I am a mournful ghost ship sailing in search of you. I keep on imagining that you are my paradise island which harbours so many memories of ecstasies and overflowing love. I keep on dreaming of taking care of you, of being the centre of yours and the children's world, of having another baby...

The last time we were together I felt like a thief: I stole from you a kiss, a reluctant smile, a passing moment of tenderness... I felt the warmth of your body, your exquisite scent, your yielding feet and even an involuntary climax. But my greatest joy was to wake up by your side and see the sky in your adorable face while dreaming of never - ever parting again.

You are my destination and at the end of this journey I shall find my anchorage, my haven for good. I sensed that you were determined to lock me away in an inaccessible part of your heart. In a supreme act of will you want to erase me from your mind and from your heart while I feel permanently encircled by you, haunted by your alluring, charming irresistible being, by your presence, but your last comforting words, by the immensity of your green dreamy eyes. You pervade me with hints from invisible worlds and reminiscences of immortality. I am sure that there is far more between us than smouldering ruins and God tells me that there is a new dawn in the horizon and that there will be a safe return to your bosom, to our children, to our better selves...

I fancy that at last I shall be returning home from a ravaging war that has come to an end. As a survivor my nightmare will only end when I would be able to hold you in my arms. I promise you that I shall be *'the shadow of your shadow'* as long as it takes for you to rediscover your buried feelings for me. I have come to grips with the quintessence of your nature and nobody can ever take your place. My passion for you springs from an inexhaustible cosmic well. I am convinced that the future bounds us together, that our children bounds us together, that love cannot be denied, that bitterness and hurt can be overcome, that we belong to each other beyond the morning star, the reverses of fortune, a passing fancy... You are wonderful beyond belief and I shall love you eternally. Not even an early grave would repel this longing for you. Please don't deprive our children of their father, don't deprive me of a life giving source, don't deprive yourself of your longest and devoted suitor, admirer, true love... I shall heal all your wounds.

I am your captive soul,

Vincent"

Thoughts On Love And Love Lost

"I am still drowning in your love. I keep on telling myself that everything ends, that time is the reef and the devourer, that I should wake up to that terrifying fact called reality, to that want of your love, to that barrenness of purpose and meaning without you. In my decline and fall you can readily identify a woman. Please, don't try too hard to blot me out, to cast me into obscurity, to treat me as your *'bête noire'* or your enemy. Why should I continue to revere, cherish and adore you in spite of your rejection? *'Red rose, proud rose, sad rose of all my days.'* (Seamus Heanney)

"I know that we have paid an enormous price for a single act of folly. When I gave myself entirely to the relationship I was derailed and shipwrecked by disaster. We share many, many wonderful and intimate moments, we are transparent to each other, I understand you more than I ever did, your moods, your affirmation of independence, your self-assertion and your needs. Have you forgotten our love pact? We are connected by an indestructible bond of sweat, blood, honey and milk.

From the deep well of love for you I am totally at your mercy. Let us start with a clean slate. I have gone astray once, I have seen the beast, I have suffered iniquity and vexation, I have fallen into a pit but nothing compares to the calamity of losing you: '...*When we are sick in fortune, often the surfeits of our own behaviour - we make guilty of our disasters the sun, the moon, and the stars; as if we were villains on necessity, fools by heavenly compulsions...*' (King Lear). You can despise me because '*I am not the master of my fate nor I am the captain of my soul*'. The future without you is like a horrifying snake-haired Gorgon. I want to be reborn for you, to win back your trust, your love, your respect, your indulgence... A poem by Matthew Arnold is my invocation to you:

'Ah, love, let us be true
To one another. For the world, which seems
to lie before us like a land of dreams,
so various, beautiful, so new.
Hath really neither joy, nor love, nor light,
nor certitude, nor peace, nor help for pain;
And we are here as on a darkling plain
Swept with confused alarms of struggle and flight,
Where ignorant armies clash by night.'

"If you knew the agony I am going through without you:
'...And she was there, my hope, my joy,
My own dear Genevieve.
I told her how he pined: and ah
The deep, the low, the pleading tone
With which I sang another's love
Interpreted my own
...And she forgave me
She wept with pity and delight,
She blushed with love
And like the murmur of a dream
I heard her breathe my name
She fled to me and wept

I calmed her fears and she was calm,
And told her love with virgin pride;
And so I won my Genevieve
My bright and beauteous bride' (S. Taylor Coleridge).

Will you forgive me or will you behave like *'La belle Dame sans merci'*?
'Oh, what can ail thee, knight at arms
Alone and palely loitering?
Oh, what can ail thee, knight at arms
so haggard and so woe-begone?
I met a lady in the meads
She took me to her elfin grot
And there she lulled me asleep
The latest dream I ever dreamed
On the cold hill's side:
'La belle Dame sans merci hath thee in thrall' (John Keats).

"I feel like Philoctetes that greek hero who had wounded himself with one of his arrows. The wound stood as well for a moral stain which yielded a stench. He was forced to travel to an isolated island where he died.
When will this debt of mine be finally paid off? Damnation can be seen as a deterrent, a branding, a nulification, a cleansing and a punishment:
'Blow, blow, thou winter wind,
Thou art not so unkind
As man's ingratitude and cruelty
Sweet are the uses of adversity,
which like a toad, ugly and venomous;
wears yet a precious jewel in his head' (Shakespeare's *'As You Like It'*).

The five year expulsion reminds me of Plato:

'...Let those who have been made what they are only from want of understanding, and not from malice or an evil nature, be placed by the judge in the sophronisterion during a period of not less than five years. And in the meantime let them have no intercourse with other citizens except with the ghosts of the sleepless nights with a view of the improvement of their soul's health. And when the time of their exclusion has expired, if they kept the soundness of mind in the years of captivity, let them be restored to sane company' (Laws, 908).

"A man may be driven away from Paradise for desobedience; he may have his Waterloo for repacious ambition or he may have his Versaille, a punitive and humiliating retribution that plant the seeds of more hatred and revanchism. Our house has been shattered by the winds of madness and the dark sea churns and swells while I wait for deliverance. We can comfort each other and ease the pain of those infamous and torturing hours. Let us sustain and nurture our love with nobility, grace and tenderness. I know that I am on trial before you but I promise I shall be:

'All made of passion, and all made of wishes
All adoration, duty and observance;
All humbleness, all patience;
All purity, all trial, all obeisance' (*'As You Like It'*).

"I don't know how to be as to please you. I might be able to read your mind, I might find a way to your heart, I might be what I once was or what you want me to be. I would like to be the wind of Malin Head, to be a sensitive high-spirited horse, to be music to your ears, to be a fellow of infinite riches, sagacity, mercy and passion, I would like to be you... How can I make you forget the last infirmity that drove us apart? I long for the affectionate beaming in your green eyes, the twinkling of your desires, your dark and fiery moments, your tears, your resolve, your beautiful and passionate body... Will I ever rise to your expectations? I thought our love was invincible. When I fear that you no longer love me I have the sensation of a void, a tumultuous abyss, quicksand under my feet and the crushing weight of time. In my solitary walks the sounds of the sea, the spirits of the woods and the whistles of the wind are my sole companions. I never dreamt of a broken home, of a fading love, of a grieving lost soul and of an ignoble end. After the seduction game, after the loving game, after the crying game and now the torture game I wish I could bask in your saintly indulgence and that you could 'suspend your disbelief' in me. Knowledge through suffering opens the possibility for real change. I know you are weary and fearful but give me a chance and with T.S. Eliot I could say: *'There is only the fight to recover what has been lost and found and lost again and again; and now, under conditions that seem unpropitious. But perhaps neither gain nor lost. For us, there is only the trying. The rest is not our business we cannot revive old factions; we cannot restore old policies; or follow an antique drum. What we call a beginning is often the end and to make an end is to make a beginning... we shall not cease from exploration and the end of all our exploring, will be to arrive where we started and know the place for the first time.'* Let bygones be bygones... In matters of the heart I was illiterate until I met you.

I am your inconsolable Orpheus who would forever play the lyre to rescue Eurydice from Hades."

"I am not the knight-errant, the dutch-errand, the jew-errant or the gypsy-errand. I am just erratic, erring in my ways, living a borrowed life and paying a heavy price for one moral failing. I experience my world framed in a chronological - conventional time, yours in a circular - recurring time and the absence of you as suspended time. Has the love we felt for each other been suffocated by my moral turpitude, my clumsiness and my gloomy disposition? To be torn away from you is like losing a part of myself. If you are able to clear from your mind 'the winter of our discontent' you will discover that we share a great deal: music, poetry, magic, travelling... Our separation has made us lose our capacity to tune in with our innermost nature.

You don't realize how sorry I feel for having brought so much grief into your life. How many times man is allowed to stumble and fall? I seem to have gone through a vortex which left me in a flutter and made your love and trust in me tumbled. Have you read that a former French minister Beregovoy committed suicide? The media got wind of the situation and unleashed a devastating campaign of calumny and innuendos directly responsible for his humiliation and sad end. The public are now attacking the media for taking the law in their own hands, for relishing in filth, for the savagery of their attack, for their one-sidedness, for the utter lack of respect for his dignity and for overlooking many other good qualities of the man. Institutions usually reflect public opinion which in turn reflect the media as shown in *'The Hidden Persuaders'*. Aldous Huxley wrote that *'one third of all human unhappiness is unavoidable while the other two thirds are created by the doomed attempt to avoid the first third'*. In this society those who fall are not necessarily the most guilty or deserving ones and not all guilty and deserving do fall. In Greek mythology Moirae is the personification of an inexorable fate which compels us back to the undifferentiation and opacity of nature. Undoubtedly, Moirae dealt a heavy blow to this former minister. Moirae also stood for Clotho who spun the thread of life, Lachesis, to whom the thread was passed as it came off the spindle and Atropos who cut it off with her shears. Do you recall when I used to help you with your knitting? Without you my life is drifting in a sea of dangers. Dangers of impotent vacillations, of fearful escapes, of exclusion, of crippling prejudices, of warped ideas, of allegiances too deeply divided... your presence put my mind to rest, you are the closest allied of nature than I ever experienced. I would like to die in your arms."

"There are so many complexities in love relationships, for instance:

Human beings are usually deeply ambivalent but a set of positive or negative feelings do prevail.

There are those who may find a person hateful although subconsciously they may be in love with her.

There are those who love when they should hate and hate when they should love as there are those who are misjudged and mistreated by the person they love and yet remain devoutedly dependent and loving.

They are those who are settling old scores with the person they believe they love.

They are those who experience in every love relationship a distorted and ghastly repetition of each former love relationship as there are those who, because of hurt feelings due to a stormy early relationship, were not able to fall in love again in the same way.

There are those whose love is ignited even more by distance and those whose love is overshadowed, benumbed or extinguished by distance.

There are those who refuse to love for fear of losing something that they prize more highly love.

They are those who feel undeserving of love or even that it is presumptuous to expect love and those who demand it with a relentless hunger and a wish to mould the chosen person in an illusory image that he is not.

They are those who can't perform sexually when they love and those who can perform sexually only when they don't love.

They are those who can only love a degraded person and those who can only love an idealized person.

They are those who can only love by substitution or by proxy while others require to find each time the difference and uniqueness in the partner.

Usually, in love relationships there is a collusion between the loser and the winner, the pursuer and the pursued, the driver and the driven, the seducer and the seduced, the victim and the victimizer. It is not always clear who does what to whom, who entices whom and whose role in the other person's mind the partner is enacting.

There are multiple components in love which are not always explicit: some are motivated by power, others by lust, others by materialistic gain, others by dependency needs, others by narcissistic supplies, others by selfless oblation or guilt...

They combine in various degrees but when there is unfulfilment or malcontent one component aggressively takes the upper hand. Love may break through the barrier of human laws, personal boundaries and decency. It is never devoid of sorrow, fictional aspects, imperfections and or an uplifting reverie."

"What is that place in your mind that you call home? This question is raised by the homeless and by those sunk to utter worthlessness and insignificance. Certainly home is not the place where the step-mother wants you dead (Hansel and Gretel), nor a place haunted by ghost, witches or other malevolent force. Home is not the place where you are not wanted nor loved. Home is that sanctuary, that virtual space within yourself, the only authentic realm where you can hide or find refuge far from 'the madding crowd' and where you can encounter the people you love the most. Home is also where you happened to be... home is in the immensity of your glance, in the hesitation of your gait, in the sumptuous dwelling of your soul and in the recesses of your irresistible body."

"At the end of the last century Oscar Wilde suffered the ultimate social humiliation and iniquity which was responsible for his downfall, exile and premature death. At the end of this century, as it was a thousand years ago, man's cruelty to man has not changed. Sometimes is better the certainty of failure that the ephemeral uncertainty of triumph. Fate is like an executioner who is about to shoot but the target is not always clean cut because his eyes are blurred. Man is usually caught between the intermittence of desire and the unknown. Free will is an mirage because God has created an imperfect being who not only deceives himself but keeps shifting his point of reference as if to shun the chaos around the corner and the emptiness yonder:

'Oh wild West wind,
Thou breath of Autumns being thou,
From whose unseen presence the leaves dead,
are driven, like ghost from an enchanter fleeing.' (Shelley)

39

I am perhaps a shadow of a shadow and you are my dream of yet another dream that somebody else dreamed.

The more things change, the more they stay the same. I am a fool, fascinated by similarities, singularities and by that which is invisible to the human eye. I was naively floating in the stream of consciousness until I hit a whirlpool which caused me to fall into the unpredictable and the chaotic. These events are not just in the realm of the metaphorical; these events such as the whims of justice, the abuse of power, the violence of totalitarian institutions, the corruption and deceit, the political winds, the crucifixion of men, the Roman circuses, the senseless tearing apart of human beings or families and the silent conspiracy of the majority are causing havoc among us.

To learn to live is to learn the limits of our prison's wall, is to learn about the sharp edge of objects and persons, its to experience the chilliness of the far side from the centre, is to have lost the point of reference or the compass and still be able, luckily, to find the harbour again and finally is to keep on hoping in spite of the relentless passage of time, the blizzard of events and the inconstancy of love.

Is love made of the stuff of dreams? Is it 'the desire of the other's desire?' Is it the actualization and embodiment of myriads of sensations since birth? Is it the reflection of our worthwhileness? Is it based on an aspiration for an object of worship? Or is it the expression of a projected fantasy that reveals the lines of fracture at the core of our beings?

You have taught me what is love, what is poetry, what is suffering, what is endurance... We are one soul and one body, we dream each other's dream, we hatch each other's children, we feel each other's sorrows, pains and distress. If I were to lose your love for ever I would feel unworthy of anybody's love because of what you represent to me. My love for you knows no bounds."

"Who is really the victim of love or of adversity? Some people are bound to ratify in reality an intrapsychic situation which is split off from their awareness. Other people search to vindicate or to avenge themselves for a wrong which was done another time by another person. Still other people inflict on somebody else the same ruthless treatment that they once received or fantasized that they had received. Interpersonal relationships are so fraught with dangers because of the ubiquity and interminability of settling past accounts and repairing old torts. That is why love relationships just as transference enactments during psychoanalysis are a minefield of unpredictable course.

The forties was the age of the holocaust and existential anxiety; the fifties the age of permissiveness; the sixties the age of revolt and protest; the seventies the age of 'artificial paradises'; the eighties the age of the limits of hedonism and sexuality because of the human immune-deficiency virus and the nineties the age of fundamentalism, purgation, feminism, exposure and vindication of the victim's role. In the film 'Damage' by Louis Malle, the victim played by Jeremy Irons is a respectable politician. Scanning the humdrum world he feels fascinated by a prototype of the 'femme fatal' who induces him into complying with her perversities. He becomes the victim's victim and yields to the forbidden, clandestine and erotic sense of aliveness that the relationship elicited in him but with lethal consequences.

Looking deep into oneself is like being a grave-digger, not knowing what skeletons are there to be found. In my opinion thanatophilia is partly a wish to return to mother-earth and to sweet oblivion. Since I left you I have nothing but the obsession of time in my mind: time is cruel, time is gold, time heals, l'eternel retour, killing time, time standing still, time flies, the inexorability of time, marking time, devouring time, timelessness, the end of times...

41

Without you I feel like a protagonist in a Samuel Beckett play: I have no source of heat, often wonder about the dissipation of bodily heat, about the fate of your love for me; I am living in uncertainty, moving for the sake of moving, drifting through the dark corridors of the mind, falling and rising with the tide of moods, waiting for Godot, feeling trapped in a timeless hole with my heart beating wildly and losing track of days or hours...but still is better to have loved and lost than never to have loved at all. What is that ambiguous border that separates naturalness, fatuity, disaffection, pride and exaggeration? Every story I hear about man is utterly familiar, it resonates painfully at the core of my being, I am an example of Job and humanity at its worst. I never experienced so much 'Weltschmerz'. When shall this nightmare end?"

"When writing to you I feel like a beggar, like a slave imploring for your benevolence and like a blind man who can only see through your eyes and feel through your heart. Love is the only protection from the tear and wear of life, from the whims of fate, from a hostile world... The shocking events has brought us in touch with the rock-bottom of life's questions. Are we meant for each other no matter what are the injuries of fate, the distance or the passage of time? We must rise above the pettiness of social injustice, material constraints, indignities, envy and hatred. It is rather easy to dissect individual along the lines prescribed by all the 'isms' and find him guilty. We are surrounded by men who like Procustes are more than willing to inflict torture on their victims and to doom them on a 'pars pro toto' judgement. Orwell's and Kafka's vision of the world, the abuse of power, the politically motivated 'witch-hunting', the incomprehensible and sudden reversal of fortunes, the scapegoatism, racism and intolerance take place even in the most advanced societies. What was unthinkable for the unsuspicious and ingenuous man now is thinkable.

After a few drinks and already somewhat inebriated I test myself by walking on tiptoes in order to recover my equilibrium. By the same token you don't know how much I wish to strike a balance with you. My favourite pastime is to evoke memories, fancies and cravings for you. Invariably, I fall in temptation and to your heart's delight I proceed to ravish you. As if, magically, by indulging in this fantasy I could induce you to overcome your current lukewarm, impervious and mindless attitude and drag you along in the dark whirlwind of passion, whispering and swooning in an embrace of rupture.

I fancy to be the West wind which caresses you and dies down in a world-deep loneliness.

Another storm 'punished' the coast with violent winds and gigantic waves that flooded the streets of the town. The fury of nature could have easily swallowed me up. Several boats were pulled out of their anchors and drifted helplessly. Indeed I felt insignificant facing the famished sea. I thought of the fragility of man, of wars, political storms, raging volcanoes or cyclones. I reflected on not having yet found a safe haven where to anchor because of my stupidity, pseudo-stupidity, masochism, asceticism or plainly ill-fate. My life appears to me like a series of discontinuous moments, of leaps and stagnations, of near catastrophes and near-triumphs. Can the case of a precipitous fall be explained in physical terms using Galileo's Law; the fall of bodies in space is the result of:

a) being at a higher level, and

b) finding oneself without support.

At times I feel like crying out, howling and crying:
'Oh God make me a mask' (Dylan Thomas).

"Symmetry is a wish to receive a reflection from the other like one would ideally like to be. In the preoccupation with symmetry there are two slants. On the one hand there is a search for a perfect equilibrium, for a twinship without dissonance on the other one encounters Blake's 'fearful symmetry' which is related to the fear of the double, the Doppelgaenger, that uncanny alter-ego that for some cultures is a premonition of death. The drive for symmetry seeks evenness, parallelism and absence of invalidating attributions or contentious conflicts. It further insist on equalization of any incompatible reality or, like in the case of horror vacuum, there is a horror of disproportions to the extend that the individual may live out and expect to find the world of persons and objects arranged in a geometrical form. It is as well a form of merging that puts out of gear and disqualifies any difference and negates the very human gap between actuality and ideality. If in the act of symmetry the other other does not reflect that idealized image one may feel nullified or deadened.

Symmetry is the basis of the alienation from oneself as well as the origin of that need to overcompensate for a psychological sense of want or a deficit. The other person who fits and complies into this required relationship feels at first indispensable. Each party may come into the relationship with a deficit or a surplus or better with deficit in some areas and surplus in others for which they are expecting complementary, fulfilment or a binding insistence to be sustained or restored. The key issue is what does the other person reflect and how do they sort out the position in space of that elusive boundary where personal identities overlapped. Being a half of another person's half one searches for completeness and occasionally for symmetry.

I have been studying the horoscope. I extracted the following observation about the Pisces woman married to an Aquarian man:

44

You are liable to find him most impractical... he is a dreamer... at times you may feel like calling it quits. Chances are that you will always give him another chance. He understands children... money burns a hole in his pocket. He is kind and generous. He will never quibble over petty things. He will encourage you to continue in your interests because he is broad-minded. It may take fifty years for him to get around to marry you but it may be worth waiting for. You should bring him down to earth when he gets too starry-eyed... In the Chinese horoscope you are a serpent and a watery sign, you are also the moon and you are my bewitching Muse. Whatever happened to your former snake charmer? He has undergone the martyrdom of his passion and was consumed by fire in love's altar.

Sometimes a dark and ominous presence is watching over me while I try to sleep but the thought of you rescues me from the unthinkable."

"I am longing to be with you. Please do not transform me into a ghost from the past. I refuse to grow vapid, dematerialize, become intangible, forgotten, kapput due to absence, shiftlessness, death or shunning. We have shared many experiences together: some sublime others sad. I am possessed by you, haunted by your presence and tortured by whatever grief I brought into your life. I have been cursed, I have seen the Furies rise, I have captured like a wretch who dared not die because of my love for you and the family. I wish my 'Golgota' would have taken place before you came into my life. On the other hand you were the only woman capable of shaking my foundations and lead me into the bowels of the earth. There is a prayer that resumes my predicament:

'I've erred and strayed from the ways like lost sheep... I've left undone those things which I ought to have done and I have done those things which I ought not to have done and there is no health in me...'

For a man like me is it true that nothing succeeds like success or the other way, especially for the believer, that nothing 'fails' like success? I am also guilty of having killed the very thing I love the most. Are you worn out and uninterested sustaining and shoring me up for such a long time? Am I responsible for an irreparable mistake? Without you I fell like a gnostic in a state of alienation and vexation. Will you ever give me a truce, flow with my feelings, abide with your feelings, abide with your taciturn lovesick slave? The root of my neurosis is an Oedipal guilt. I was my mother's favourite and she devoted much of her energies to nurturing and educating me. She made me feel so special that I knew in my heart that I was for her more important than my father. I had the conviction, as I succeeded in everything I tried, that he was a defeated and displaced man. Even his orders were usually overruled by mother. I knew that sooner or later I had to pay a price for having surpassed my father and, no wonder, because my tribulations started shortly after his death. After the fall, the weaker I became the stronger you grew; the more shortcomings I appeared to have the more you scintillated with virtues; the more dependent and clinging I became the more you wanted to be self-reliant, to get rid of 'a dead weight', of a looser and to be independent. You did not consider that both aspects of that equation are as much part of you as they are part of me. Now you seem to identify with the most cunning, forthright and able part of each of your parents. You have the ability to be 'mother hen' and have sided with your mother in undermining your overbearing and self-righteous father while at the same time you identify with him as the aggressor and become wilful and dominant like him. The difference between your father and me is that he kept the reigns of power, was an unrepentant womanizer and at that he was impregnated with machism and even though he was not popular or lovable he never experienced a calamitous fall. Your mother accumulated a heap of resentment against him and commissioned her daughters into complicity and duplicity with the purpose of thwarting and out-manoeuvring the man. The submission of your mother was only apparent. She really used her daughters as an effective weapon. You often said that you could never be married to a man like your father. Or perhaps you have not yet vindicated you mother for the sufferings your father inflicted on her. It is so strange that I am identifying with your world of fantasies: your favourite fantasies are being at the mercy of person, being forced into submission, into bondage and thralldom. Whatever happens to you in these fantasies is the result of being overpowered for which you have no control or responsibility. Like St Paul I am possessed by an indomitable, irrepressible and irresistible love for you that has become my religion."

"Mircea Eliada refers to the modern man utterly defenceless submitted to 'the terror of history', those inexorable events sweeping him in a deforming mass that transcend his individuality. According to the Hindu world view every man is born with a debt, his karma, and the freedom to incur new debts. This invariably defines his particular karmic equation: a burden of cosmic, psychological or historical sufferings, blows and injustices that had remained unresolved from previous lives. James Joyce and T.S. Eliot show that gnawing nostalgia for the return of the past and the ubiquitous wish to abolish time. I believe it was Tolstoy who attributed to that 'weather condition' called 'love' much of the suffering of men. Love carries man to the limits of the human condition. It ennobles and elevates him but also causes him to disgrace himself, to cut a sorry figure, to betray his closest friend, to fall from a high estate, and even may bring about scandal and dishonour. The Scholastics understood love in three different senses:

a) Sensual love, amor complacentiae et concupiscentiae which may lead to thralldom (Sklaverei, Gefangenschaft) and passion (Leidenschaft sich hinreissen lassen). Love in the sense of desire is to be needed, to be 'starved' for affection, to covet, to cling to and to feel greedy. The Greek goddess of love Aphrodite spread her favours lustfully and liberally but during Plato's time a spiritualized form and a more degraded one called Porne (the 'titillator') was known.

b) Amor benevolentiae et beneficentiae based on generosity, kindness, charity and disinterestedness.

c) Amor unionis based on the principle that 'amare est gaudere felicitate alterious', to love is to rejoice in the happiness of the other. True love implies self-abnegation, self denial and commitment. (Selbstentsagung, Selbstlos, Selbstverleugnung) akin to devotion and faith (voellige Eingabe an Gott). 'True love is a variety of self-surrender, idealization and a form of getting lost and losing oneself in the enigma of the other. When the love for the eternal feminine is not involved, a father may express love for his children as if he is part of a whole and decisively would show preference for their interests ahead of his'. True love projects us beyond conceit, self-conceit, vanity and self-love (Eigenliebe, l'amour-prôpre).

In every love relationship there is an 'Invocation to Echo':
'Sweet Echo, sweetest Nymph,
That liv'st unseen
Within thy airy shell,
By slow Meander's margent green,
And in the violet-embroider'd vale,
Where the love-lorn nightingale
Nightly to thee her sad song mourneth well;
Canst thou not tell me of a gentle pair

That likest thy Narcissus are?
O, if thou have
Hid them in some flowery cave,
Tell me but where,
Sweet queen of parley, daughter of the sphere.
So may'st thou be translated to the skies,
And give resounding grace to all Heaven's harmonies'
(*Milton's Minor Poems* - Selected by O, Smeaton - Robert Scott - London).

In French *'L'amour propre'*, basically a selfish, self-seeking and self-indulgent orientation (Selbstsuechtig), must be distinguished from *'l'amour de soi'* which signifies an instinct for self-preservation and self-respect.

It is rather infrequent to remain fixated in a particular form of love but generally a set of feelings and a disposition prevails within a particular relationship. For instance Victor Hugo in his writings emphasized his fascination and wish to rescue fallen women. Others may be attracted by the forbidden or by the duplicity of parallel lives. Generally, these men (homo duplex) are ridden with a conflict between dream and reality, action and intention, the ideal and the real, one side competing and displacing the other at different times in different settings.

Freud distinguished between sacred and profane love and between being in love as fascination and being in love as bondage. In the first case the ego has enriched itself with the properties of the object. In the second case it has surrendered itself to the object, it has impoverished (itself Group Psychology and Analysis of the Ego vol. XVIII of the Standard Edition), *On Narcissism* (vol.XIV) and *A Special Type of Choice of Object Made by Men* (vol. XI) are Freud's most revealing tests on the psychology of love. For example one can easily think of men who require for a woman to be married in order to seduce or to fall in love with her. As in the film

'The Blue Angel' based on Heinrich Mann's story, Professor Unrat falls in love with a 'cocotte' which spells his downfall. In some of Somerset Maughan's novels there is a drive in men to rescue fallen women. Man cannot escape his 'demon' as Freud pointed out in his text *'The Universal Tendency to Debasement in the Sphere of Love'* (vol.XI): *'They seek objects which they do not need to love in order to keep their sensuality away from the objects they love and where they desire they do not love'* (p.183). In *'The Taboo of Virginity'* (The Standard Edition, vol.XI) Freud traces the state of bondage to *'whoever is the first to satisfy a virgin desire for love long and laboriously held in check'* (p.193) and further: *'As often as they try to direct their love toward some other man, the image of the first although he is no longer loved intervenes with inhibiting effect... They cannot get away from them because they have not completed their revenge upon them...'* (p.208). Freud invokes Judith castrating Holofernes who has deflowered her to support his argument. It cannot be argued of a halo effect of the first major infatuation but to reduce it to the loss of virginity is a gross simplification. As there are women who may overestimate their virginity there are those whose sexuality is used as a weapon in a search for conquest. Freud in *'Observations on Transference Love'* writes:

'There is, it is true, one class of woman with whom this attempt to preserve the erotic transference for the purpose of analytic work without satisfying it will not succeed. These are women of elemental passion who tolerate no surrogates. They are children of nature who refuse to accept the psychical in place of the material who, in the poet's word, are accessible only to 'the logic of soup, with dumplings for arguments'. With such women one has the choice between returning their love or else bringing down upon oneself the full enmity of a woman scorned' (vol.XII, pp.166-167).

"I have been guilty of being gullible and on putting too much faith in human beings. I have never learned properly to be guarded, to deny, to watch out for snares, baits and meshes, to suspect human motives, to protect myself from the snake in the grass, from the diabolic and the wicked in the world and to have a measure of foresight when feeling bruised. Some of my friends are of the opinion that this incapacity for self-defence or self-care was at the root of my downfall. You have been my guiding light in the dark labyrinth of the nightmarish years. You are so precious and unique that I refuse to give you up even if what is left is an 'agalma' (that very special, illuminated, ornate and gorgeous object of desire), a fantasy of a fantasy, the spectre of the rose, a sign of a sign pointing to you, a void. I am inhabited by you, by your speech, by your gestures and your demeanour.

'And I stood in a strange enchantment,
I had known it all before:
In my heart of hearts was the magic
Of days that will come no more,
The magic of joy departed,
That Time can never restore.
That never, ah, never, never,
Never again can be:
Shall I tell you what powerful fairy
Built up this palace for me?
It was only a little white violet
I found at the root of a tree' (Adelaide A. Procter).

Our relationship or what remains of it can also be seen from another point of view: one side of you had always had the wish to be deeply feminine, traditional and cared for. You wanted to depend and lean on a strong and totally trustworthy man. I don't really believe in this male-female stereotype, but they seem to be imprinted in our culture for better or for worse. Throughout my letters I elevated you to the quintessence of femininity, of devotion and of the cycles of nature. This dream of yours was in conflict with your wish for autonomy, self-affirmation, independence and your career ambitions. The awareness of this conflict, brought into the open by my downfall, became a source of great anxiety for both of us as was our concern with the hiatus between seeming and being. As I became enfeebled, unmanly and impoverished you took it as an affront to your feminine yearnings for protection, security and dependability. Women never seem to forgive the failures of their partners. You don't really believe in Virgil's dictum: *'Forgive the vanquished and humble the arrogant'* (Parcere subiectis et debellare superbos)? Your image of me had become eroded and downgraded. You had to take over functions that imposed a burden on you. Your artistic, feminine and contemplative wishes had to be suppressed and you had to become a doer while I drifted into nomadic existence.

I shall never be able to extricate myself from the 'fearful symmetry' that draws me to you. Will the avenging Eumenides triumph over love? Will I be condemned to quell my sorrow, to quench my thirst and to sink in a speechless silence with God as my only consolation. Paradoxically, now that I have attained higher spirituality and, even by your own yardstick, I have improved in many dimensions, you reject me. Now that I have come around to meet some of your exacting expectations you don't want me any more. Now that I am transparent and absolutely sincere you close your mind. Much of these changes in me, I must admit, came as a result of the annihilating blows and the agony of finding my way out of hell. My treasure, have faith in our future and we shall overcome fate and odium and we shall dispel this sorry scheme of things. Even if you show contempt for me I'll remain you slave and patiently shall wait for the day when you'll open to me the innermost recesses of your heart."

"Our destinies are interlocked in more than one way: 'triste vagaba en la vida hasta que llegaste tu'. After talking to you on the phone I had the lingering hope that there is a censor in you not allowing that loving and forgiving side of yours to yield to the temptation of taking me back; that censor appears to suppress any twinkle of feelings for me and does not wish to let me enter into your life even through a backdoor. I have known you for centuries and have discerned every aspect of your luxuriant personality. I had bathed in the beauty of your soul, I had awakened you when you were the Sleeping Beauty in more than one respect, I had suffered your indifference and now I must come to grips with the Beast in the Beauty or with the Beauty and the Beast.

'O Rose, thou art sick.
The invisible worm
That flies in the night,
In the howling storm,
Has found out thy bed
Of crimson joy;
And his dark secret love
Does thy life destroy' (William Blake).

When the thorn of a red rose pricked my finger I fell in a state of despair over our future together... a drop of blood, a pact that was broken, the parting of ways, ashes and nostalgia... Human beings are so strange. It appears that the more the love a person had experienced the more the unforgiveness and cruelty he is capable of expressing after the last act of betrayal.

Women who succumb to the deepest infatuation are the most capable of barbaric, cruel and tantalizing acts of vengeance.

I am terrified of losing you forever before being able to win you back and make you really happy at least for the last stretch of my life. That old black magic of yours has me enthralled. I enjoyed reading the book of Ghyslain Charron about Piera Aulagnier who distinguishes passion from love not only on a quantitative but also on a qualitative basis. In the passionate state, an asymmetrical relationship is established while being in love is a symmetrical and reciprocal relationship. In excess, however, that drive for symmetry may reach frightful proportions to the extend of imposing on the relationship a symmetry that becomes a house of mirrors:

'Tiger, tiger burning bright
In the forests of the night,
What immortal hand or eye
Dare frame thy fearful symmetry?' (William Blake).

Normally, a symmetrical relationship implies sharing or an illusion of sharing even though there may not be an equal libidinal investment on either part: *'Divisé entre le souhait de rompre et le désir de maintenir la relation amoureuse, plus d'un individu espère rompre, hésite à le faire, anticipe avantages et inconvénients, décide en pensée, manque de courage pour agir, se dégoûte de sa faiblesse, se plaint et gémit, part, revient, menace de partir encore...puis attend la mort..celle de l'autre, la sienne, comme la seule véritable chance de voir se dénouer le conflit amoureux, et encore, puisque la mort de l'un peut susciter chex le survivant une blessure que dure autant que lui...'* (p.194). In passion the individual is seized or overcome by the object of desire and is lifted to a state of inebriation where love, jealousy, suffering, pleasure and 'jouissance' intertwine... *'La passion du toxicomane pour sa drogue, la passion du joueur pour le jeu, la passion du Je pour un autre sujet, autant d'exemples qu'elle regroupe dans une meme categorie, celle de la relation passionnelle. L'objet de la passion est 'un objet non substituable, un objet nécessaire parce qu'il repond a un désir qui est devenu un besoin'* and a exclusive source of every pleasure. (p.195)... *'la pierre de touche n'est pas 'je jouis, donc j'aime, 'mais plutot 'je souffre, donc j'aime'* (p.196)... *'Le 'coup de foudre' se présente a lui, tel un éblouissement qui l'arrache à la banalité de la vie ordinaire, et le jette sans rémission vers l'objet idéalisé'* (p.198) (Ghyslain Charron: *Le Discours et le Je-La Theorie de Piera Aulagnier* - Les Presses de l'Université Laval-Klincksieck, Paris, 1993).

The passionate man lives in turbulence, vehemence, *'Sturm und Drang'* and at times volcanic frenzy. Eventually passion consumes itself and is or is not replaced by love which is a restless and continual striving for the unknowable and unattainable in the other. Max Scheler pointed out that true love does not arise from pity or sympathy, nor is a desire to improve the love object nor is based on admiration or esteem for the qualities of the loved object. Often is difficult to justify the choice of the love object since another person with whom I am not in love may have all or more qualities than the person of my choice. We are also aware since Plato and Aristotle that a good and worthy person is more likely to inspire love than a villain, a fallen angel, a bully or a castaway but this is not always the case. For Christianity the unworthy man, the lost sheep, the sinner is most worthy of love because he needs to be rescued and redeemed.

Moirae, my love for you is hopelessly romantic since I cherish your uniqueness as something incomparable and irreplaceable. My love for you is like a Madonna worship, my love for you is blind, my love for is 'clairvoyant'...

'My bounty is as boundless as the sea,
My love as deep: the more I give to thee
The more I have, for both are infinite'
                                   (Shakespeare's *Romeo and Juliet*).

I shall keep on wandering the deserts, the plains and the mountains looking for you and even when I realize that I am already long dead I shall keep on looking for you. I seem to reverberate, to hum, to twitter, to rehearse the unlimited moments of sharing we had in the past (Mitfreude, Mitleid, Mitmachen, Mitreden und Mitschuld). Since I met you I seem to have actualized a higher value (Hoeherseins des Wertes). I seem to have seen beyond your personal magnetism, sensuality and poetry and have discovered a world in itself, a universe, a palpitating humanity and a timeless archetype. You have no idea of the torment I go through not being able to be at your side.

Nowhere I would rather be than beside you:
'Lonelies the sad
Haunters of Perhaps
Who estranged and aloof
...Brood over being till,
The bar closes' (Auden).

Scheler in *'Form and Essence of Sympathy'* - points out that often man does not suspect his worth until he is loved or until he is in love even without being reciprocated in his love. Love is not based on the actual value of the object of love, as others know her, but on the magnetism and sway that the person is capable of eliciting and the new sense of value and possibilities it brings about. In the state of being in love we must navigate between Plenty and Poverty (Plato), the former standing for the flight of imagination, creativity and feelings and the latter for the short-sighted actuality the couple is constrained to encounter in the real world. We would agree that selfless love, self-sacrifice and empathy (Einfuehlung) have become a rare event in our smug, indolent, loveless and hedonistic world. The subjective experience of the other (Analogieschluss) is at the heart of loving feelings. The lover wants to be in 'speaking terms' with the beloved, with Nature, with the Cosmos. The lover searches Thou-ness (Du-heit) and his love, hopes and fears are projected onto an imperfect, incomplete world and, not infrequently, from there onto a holy and divine 'screen'. In love one discovers the knowledge of essences, the astonishment that something is rather than is not, the difference between becoming (das Werdende) and what has become (das Gewordene) and the ideal contrasting with the actual.

Lee Van Dovski in his book *'La Erotica De Los Genios'*: Genie und Eros (Published by Santiago Rueda, Buenos Aires, 1947) studied the amorous life of creative geniuses. The height of inspiration afforded by the state of being in love to men like Goethe, Byron and Shelley contrasts with the aesthetics of the morbid, the pathological and the uncanny in desperados who write about the darkest underground of the soul such as Hoelderlin, Poe, Strindberg and Baudelaire.

In Goethe poise and passion are harmonious:
'Du hast uns oft im Traum gesehen
Zusammen zum Altare gehen
Und dich als Frau und mich als Mann;
Oft nahm ich wachend deinem Munde
In einer unbewachten Stunde
So viel man Kuesse nehmen kann
Sie sind, die suess vertrauemten Stunden,
Die durchgekuessten sind verschwunden,
Wie wuenschen traurig sie zurueck...'
'Traeumte da von allen goldnen Stunden

Ungemischter lust,
Hatte schon dein liebes Bild empfunden
Tief in meiner Brust.
Bin ich's noch, den du bei so viel Lichtern
An dem Spieltisch haeltst?
Oft so unertraeglichen Gesichtern
Gegenueber stellst?
Reizender is mir des Fruehlings Bluete
Nun nich auf de Flur;
Wo du, Engel, bist, ist Lieb' und Guete
Wo du bist, Natur.'

'Sag, was will das Schicksal uns bereiten?
...Kanntest jeden Zug meinem Wesen,
Spaehtest, wie die reinste Nerve klingt,
konntest mich mit einem Blicke lesen
Den so schwer ein sterblich Aug durchdringt,
Tropftest Maessigung dem heissen Blute,
Richtetest den wilden irren Lauf,
Und in deinen Engelsarmen ruhte
Die zerstoerte brust sich wieder auf.'

In Mallarme's *'Regilla'* the waiting becomes despairing:
'...Hanté du souvenir de sa forme charmante,
L'Epoux désesperé se lament et tourmente
La pourpre sans sommeil du lit d'ivoire et d'or.
Il tarde. Il ne vient pas. Et l'âme de l'Amante,
Anxieuse, espérant qu'il vienne, vole encore
Autour du sceptre noir que leve Rhadamanthe'
  (Poesies, vol.5, Editions Barnard & Westwood, London).

In Annabel Lee, Poe's necrophilic yearnings are pathetic:

'...A wind blew out a cloud by night
Chilling my Annable Lee;
So that her highborn kinsmen came
And bore her away from me,
To shut her up in a sepulchre
In this kingdom by the sea.
...But our love it was stronger by far than the love
Of those who were older than we -
Of many far wiser than we -
And neither the angels in Heaven above
Nor the demons down under the sea,
Can ever dissever my soul from the soul
Of the beautiful Annabel Lee: -
For the moon never beams without bringing me dreams
Of the beautiful Annabel Lee;
And the stars never rise but I see the bright eyes
Of the beautiful Annabel Lee;
And so, all the night-tide, I lie down by the side
Of my darling, my darling, my life and my bride,
In her sepulchre there by the sea -
In her tomb by the side of the sea'.

And in *'The Raven'* Poe writes in a similar lugubrious tone:

'...Ah, distinctly I remember it was the bleak December
And each separate dying ember wrought its ghost upon the
floor.
Eagerly I wish the morrow; - vainly I had to borrow
From my books surcease of sorrow - sorrow for the lost
Lenore -
For the rare and radiant maiden whom the angels name
Lenore -
Nameless here for ever more...'

(*The American Tradition in Literature* vol.1-4th edition. Edited by S. Bradley, R.C. Beatty, E. Hudson Long and G. Perkins. Grosset and Dunlap, USA, 1974.)

That haunting familiar face of the beloved is incomparably portrait in Verlaine's *'Mon Rêve Familier'*:

'Je fais souvent ce rêve étrange et pénétrant
D'une femme inconnue, et que j'aime, et qui m'aime,
Et qui n'est, chaque fois, ni tout a fait la même
Ni tout a fait une autre, et m'aime et me comprend...
Car elle me comprend, et mon coeur transparent
Pour elle seule, helas cesse d'être un probleme
Pour elle seule, et les moiteurs de mon front blême,
Elle seul les sait refraichir, en pleurant...'(*Poemes Saturniens* - Le Livre de Pôche, Paris 1961).

Van Dovski commenting on the book of Flaubert *'November'* identified six motives for artistic creativity; a) a wish to upgrade one's self-esteem and to compensate for an inferiority complex; b) a wish to resolve the enigma of the other sex; c) a longing to know one self and to solve one's conflicts; d) a wish to perpetuate one's state of being in love which may be an idealizing and surprising creative act; e) nostalgia for a lost paradise and a flight from reality into a world of fantasy, and f) a flagrant opposition between the ego and the world. I can identify myself with each of these motives and would add a couple more such as a wish to make reparation for real or imagined acts of aggression and a Pygmalion complex (the sculptor who created such a beautiful sculpture that he fell in love with it). Eventually Aphrodite felt sorry for him and gave life to his creation. It shows the ubiquity of narcissism in the state of love.

All what has taken place in our life has opened the gates of the Aesthetic, the Ethical, the Speculative and the Religious levels of Existence in Kierkegaard's sense. Before the catastrophic events I couldn't go beyond the Aesthetic and the Speculative. Man may get lost in that transitional space without being able to make a 'leap of faith' that would deliver him from bondage to his beloved. As love elevates a person to the heights of thoughts and the depths of feelings also may plunge him into despair and madness. Often, there is nothing to be done except to wait for the transfiguration of the 'total occupation' of the soul by the palpitating loveliness, a process akin to mourning, and for him to re-find that gem of authenticity which he had experienced in the past. Freud remarked that the prototype of every love relationship is the baby at the mother's breast. There can be little doubt that the most gripping love relationship represent a maternal image in its various forms, la femme fatal, part of man's feminine side, an 'unreachable star', 'the garden of delights', an undeciphered dream within a dream and the abyss of being to which gladly he would leap. Would Moirae dare to look at what is concealed, latent, out of sight, shadowy and misty within her? There she would probably find a truer, inviolate, pristine and magic self still relating to Vincent who writes to her: *'I know that you are the most important person in my life, that I fathom you everywhere, that life is not worth living without the hope of reunion and that whatever crisis we went through the wounds can be healed. My whole purpose in life is to be there for you, to take care of you and to die in your arms. We have a pact of blood. Let us not challenge the scheming fates. These profusion of words were written in the dimness and coldness of lonely nights far away from your fugitive love.'*

61

"The complexity of human beings rests on the contradictiveness of its nature:

'I know my soul hath power to know all things,
Yet she is blind and ignorant in all:
I know I'm one of Nature's little kings
Yet to the least and vilest things I'm thrall.
I know my life's a pain and but a span;
I know my sense is mock'd in everything;
And, to conclude, I know myself a Man -
Which is a proud and yet a wretched thing' (Sir John Davies cited in T.S. Eliot: *On poetry and Poets*, Faber and Faber, London, 1957)."

Man is essentially divided and torn between an authentic and a false self, between moral principles in conflict with his darker side and between a self trying to live up to his own conflicting or impossible demands and a self trying to adapt to an often hostile and inclement outer world where he finds no shelter. Erich Fromm in *'Escape From Freedom'* noted that modern life breeds a feeling of fear, insecurity, powerlessness and insignificance that defensively engenders rituals, compulsions and self-restraints which prevent the individual from using his freedom. We went through the silent generation, the lost generation, the age of the subversive, the age of anxiety, the age of the machine, the need for security at any price, the affectless numbness of numbers and figures, the industry of death, the countless cases of man's inhumanity to man and we are still no better than in the past.

In the state of being in love one can observe the varieties of human self-deception, cruelty to one's fellow being, disgruntled doubts and failed idealization. Captivity in love, the inevitability of long reproachful silences, restless demons within human erring follow an fateful course. At the root of failure of couples is the fact that their interaction may be largely uplifting or degrading. Each of these multiplicities of interactions are registered in a reservoir of loveability or self-worth. When the debasement of that actual self and its ideal image predominates it may cause an erosion in the very foundation of love: 'the desire of the Other's desire', to feel lovable is to reflect each other's acceptance and goodness. There are many couples who live happily together until they decide to marry and from then on the relationship may take a downhill course. There are so many fantasies associated to the state of being married some positive, others negative depending on the past history of each person.

Freud introduced the Oedipal complex as a landmark of development. Based on this archetype men have a tendency to split women into the Madonna or mother type and the Prostitute type (Dirne) which causes them to find the Dirne, vamp or femme fatal more exciting than their own loving wife. That is why the tender and the sensual components of love may remain separate. This split is probably related to an earlier one between the good and the bad mother, the fairy godmother and the witch, the angelic woman and the Hag or Jezebel, etc.

Another conditions of love (Liebesbedingung) pointed out by Freud is that the woman who is the object of desire be married, that she belongs to another man or is tainted by disrepute. The right to 'jouissance' increases with the transgression and the fear of betrayal. She is the woman of others. For some men there are many complicated requirements for falling in love, some are conscious and others are unconscious. The price we are willing to pay for the love object (its value or Wert) is determined by the Other, the competing party. There may be overestimation or debasement of the object of love which is closely related to the person's degree of self-esteem and that internalized Other (the superego) that burdens us with pitiless guilt. Long before we find that special object of love, under the conditions that fascinate us most, we already are familiar with those traits, those divine features, that irresistible allurement that eventually take hold of us at a fateful moment when filled with uncertainties while sailing between the Scylla and Charybdis of this world we become anxious to anchor in terra firma (Tyche).

While for Freud love is based on repetition (to find a love object is in fact to re-find it) and substitutions for Lacan and particular for Jacques-Alain Miller in his *'Logic of Amorous Life'*. (Publisher Manantial Press, Buenos Aires, 1991) love is an attempt at inventing a symbolic Other. (Lacan's 'desire is the desire of the Other's desire' and Racine's: *'Rentre dans le Neant d'où je t'ai fait sortir')*.

For Lacan love like transference is essentially a lure, a trompe-l'oeil, a porte-parole that reveals what is not and hides what it is. Its space of play and amusement is the looking glass and the mirror in the realm of the imaginary or narcissistic small other (a):

'Dante once prepared to paint an angel:
Whom to please? You whisper 'Beatrice'...
You and I would rather see that angel,
Painted by the tenderness of Dante,
Would we not? - than read a fresh Inferno' (Robert Browning).

For Lacan there is an interplay of the capital Other (Autre) with a bar (A̶), the capital Other (A) without a bar and the small other (a). The obsessional lover attempts to deny the desire of the Other (with the bar) and puts in its place a polished ideal Other. The hysterical lover attempts to identify with the fault of the Other (with the bar) which leads to 'jouissance' but not the desire of the Other. The fetishistic lover, by a process of substitution of the penis, fabricates a screen object (e.g. the glance or shine on the nose, the feet) and identifies with it. The psychotic lover is, without defences, inhabited by language and at the mercy of the 'jouissance' of the Other.

We have emphasized the importance of projective identification (a narcissistic defence) in the interaction between lovers. Whether love is repetition and its wider Nietzschean frame of the 'Eternal Return', an invention, a satanic descent in terms of Sartre's *'L'Enfer c'est les autres'* or Shakespeare's *'Love's Labour's Lost'* it shakes our very foundation of being. There are other causes of disruption and division: a party may use predominantly repression (Verdraengung) and or suppression of the inner life while the other may use splitting (Verwerfung, Forclusion) or disavowal and denial (Verneinung, Verleugnung). The opportunity for interpersonal conflicts does not only arise from compatibility, complementarity and tolerance but it comes from the particular type of past relationship which has been evoked or activated and the defences it mobilized to cope with the affective storms generated by these intrapsychic events. The object small 'a' that illusory captivating make-believe fantasy object, undergoes a process of wasting in the imaginary order and does not enter in the chain of signifiers while the object Other (A) or the ego-ideal enters in the realm of the symbolic order. While Dante found in Beatrice the unique, the absolute symbolic Other (closer to the idea of God) for most humans love is an entrapment in the imaginary or narcissistic order.

A voyage is undertaken by the restive person from a state of need to the demand to an Other that satisfies it which in turn inflames the desire. From there another demand is formulated to an Other that does not satisfy the desire and after many detours he finds the road to 'la jouissance'. Like the object small o (a) 'la jouissance' does not enter into the chain of signifiers and derives from the renunciation of the drives (Triebverzicht) and the formation of the superego. In the final analysis there is an apportionment of guilt were is due and an understanding that the more the guilty feelings, the more the sadistic components of the superego and the more the 'jouissance'. The sense of morality is therefore supported by the renunciation of the drives, by 'la jouissance' that results from this renunciation and by the requirement to sacrifice the self for the sake of an ideal. The paradox is that the person may enjoy more in relinquishing his drives than in fulfilling them because of that deadly and blind craving for 'la jouissance'. Another paradox is the more a man becomes an impeccable master of himself the more he becomes a slave of himself.

Freud distinguished the narcissistic love based on sameness and similarity (I love myself in the reflection of the other) from the anaclitic love based on dependency needs (Hilflosigkeit, Abgaengigkeit). Narcissistic love, and its varieties in the quest for symmetry and perfection, engenders a state of overestimation, mirroring, reciprocity and completion of the self which is likely to become precarious and bound to fissure or fragmentation. The recipient of narcissistic love sooner or later fails to live-up to the idealization. The reservoir of narcissistic libido can be directed to the other, to the body or to the self. La Rochefoucauld was well aware of this type of love when he wrote: *'Il n'y a point de passion où l'amour de soi-même règne si puissamment que dans l'amour; et on est toujours plus disposé a sacrifier le repos de ce qu'on aime qu'à perdre le sien"* (p.67, *Maximes et Reflexions*, Editions Gallimard, 1965).

Anaclitic love is more likely to induce fear of object loss (Angst von der liebesverlust). The recipient of anaclitic love

66

may have such an inordinate degree of unmet dependency needs. Both type of losses may be aggravated by the fear of loss of the self which in the narcissistic type with its blurring of boundaries may be the loss of the extension of the self accompanied by reactive narcissistic rage and in the dependency type the loss of the nurturing other with reactive aggression. The demand for love may be addressed to an Other that does not have what is solicited or to an Other that does have it. As mentioned above, Eros was the son of Poros (exuberant resources) and Penia (want and privation): it promises far more than what it delivers. In love there is also a sharp distinction, not always maintained, between ownership and possession (seating on), masquerading and being.

The fear of loss of love without becomes the fear of the extinction of love within (aphanisis); then, there is the fear of the loss of meaning and the fear of dead itself (thanatophobia versus thanatophilia). Beyond a transgression there is always a mirror that reflects our actions.

Generally, when we are in love we seek to surpass conflicts, overcome differences, conceal our flaws, create a screen of mystification and participate in a superior and transcendent world where fiction and reality are interlaced. But the more stormy the passion the more we are lifted to the heights of desire, particularly, when a third alluring party is lurking in the dark or the woman titillate our doubts:

'I told my love, I told my love,
I told her all my heart;
Trembling, cold in ghastly fears,
Ah, she doth depart.
Soon as she was gone from me,
A traveller came by,
Silently, invisibly -
O, was no deny' (Dante Gabriel Rossetti).

Love can also cause us to plunge in the most oblique and shameless degradation. Women who fall in love with a man of reputation, wealth or power quickly fall out of love if he happens to lose them. Usually, a person finds the partner he deserves but not unusually he may succumb to a partner he does not deserve. Contrary to the reality principle, this obvious unsuitability may inflame even more the passion and longings:

'A Fathomless and Boundless deep,
There we wander, there we weep;
On the hungry craving wind
My Spectre follows thee behind.
...Dost thou not in Pride and Scorn
Fill with tempests all my morns,
And with jealousies and fears
Fill my pleasant nights with tears?' (Dante Gabriel Rossetti).

"The capacity to love may go through periods of obliteration, fading or extinction which Ernest Jones calls the aphanisis of desire. Writing then becomes a way of inventing a world in the place of a void and an absence. But the writer becomes entangled in his own dreams and while he searches for the meaning of love he experiences the unutterable effacement of meaning. Then he is sustained not by love but by words that point to it. Invariably he realizes that what is left out is more important than what is written. There is always an abysmal gap between the wish and its realization. The last time I left you I did not really leave you. I was there reliving, reviving and re-inventing every single interaction of ours. Some day, perhaps, I will leave for good but, no doubt, I will be left with a fracture in my soul, the bitter taste of your absence and the haunting sweet aroma of your presence."

"I am trying to find a way out of my interminable bondage to you, to your eyes, to your body, to that crypt of joy, to that sanctum of delectation, to your many demonstrations of rancour or love, to the thousands memories accumulated during our long attachment... but no matter how much you flaunt your lover while I wait for you or cook your dinner, no matter how much you reject me, how much you torment me, how much you dash my hopes, how much you show me utter cruelty, hostile silence or occasionally pity I am still hopelessly in love with you. After Dostoyevsky had spent his passion in love he became a compulsive gambler and married a second time at the ripe age of forty seven a girl of twenty, Ana Grigorievna who, wilfully, rectified his life in more than one way. Nobody as Dostoyevsky could be more human, more reckless, more of a transgressor, a wretch, a lost sheep... and yet at the same time he was deeply impregnated with spirituality, charity and Agapé (*'Cartas De Dostoyevsky A Su Mujer'* - 1867-1880; translated by N.S. Palenicia -Editorial Apolo, Barcelona, 1944).

You talk of your faithfulness to me up to recent times. On my part, with the exception of one act of folly, in reaction to the threat of losing you, I have been totally faithful and unmitigatingly in love with you. In regard to that act of folly of mine early in our relationship: do you recall writing to me those 'riot act' letters where you judged me as inadequate and useless 'except in bed' and threatened to terminate the relationship unless I would comply with a number of conditions. I reacted with outrage, a sense of abandonment, despair, jealousy (thinking that you already had found a replacement) and made a terrible blunder for which I was going to pay the rest of my life. There is some degree of madness in passionate love but invariably one finds a kernel of historical truth (and a degree of reason based on non-verbal clues) in this temporary insanity as is the case of the grip of jealousy, the helplessness of bondage and the fear of acting perverse fantasies. I found in Rochefocauld a definition of jealousy, *'La jalousie ne subsiste que dans les doutes; l'incertitude es sa matière; c'est une passion qui cherche tous les jours de nouveaux sujets d'inquiétude et de nouveaux tourments; on cesse d'être jaloux dès que l'on est éclairci de ce que causait la jalousie'* (p.31) (*'La Rochefoucauld - Maximes et Reflexions'* Editions Gallimard, 1965)."

The more a man pursues the cultural stereotype of a feminine ideal (e.g. an alluring, delicate, fragile, sweet, enchanting, cryptic and veiled type) the more he is bound to be led astray into a fictitious world. There are people who no matter what you do for them they cannot be grateful or satisfied. They look constantly for an external source of pleasure and are devoid of compensatory fantasies to make up for external deficiencies. They often live on borrowed psychological supplies and attention. There is a dependency and a weakness which forces the other to be the caretaker at least for the time being. Other couples may also sustain a compensatory or complementary balance in their relationship, for example: an hysterical woman who relies on feelings and screen fantasies and a obsessive man who relies on hard core evidence and thoughts; a woman with masculine traits and a self-effacing, timid and effeminate male; a maternal woman and a dependent man; an aggressive and dominant male and a guilt-ridden, masochistic female; a sex-driven and a sex-avoidant person and so on.

In psychoanalysis there is a well studied defence mechanism called projective identification which consists in inducing the other party to act out a role, to materialize a self-fulfilling prophesy, an unconscious script or a not so unconscious but

70

shared fantasy. In the long run, one party may start to feel or act in a manner concurrent with that fantasy. We have all experienced that during a particular interaction we may feel lifted, exalted, bewildered, downgraded or placed in a bind to act out a role in the other's fantasy. Each person's role responsiveness may lead him to engage in self-defeating interactions and this further contribute to the partner's conflicts. Another source of joy or jealousy, inclusion or exclusion for the man is the birth of a child. Often the man is merely a way for the woman to get a child. What is the fate of her love for him after the child is born? That will certainly depend on the father's reactions and the mother's degree of symbiosis with the baby that may shut out the partner. That baby may also have a role in the mother's fantasies and may represent a person of her past.

We chase after a dream, a trait, or a shadowy form and have to invent or re-invent the rest: the adornment, the dressing and the finery but, sometimes, we project our worst fantasies on that unsuspecting person which becomes untenable when we pressure that very person to collude or comply with our world of fantasies. It occurs frequently in love relationship to the extend that one partner may end up feeling or behaving like the father or the mother of the other partner or start believing that he is what he is not. The mother trying to mould the baby in keeping with her fantasies and a partner trying to make the partner fit into his expectations and fantasies are examples of the power of projective identification. The hold, the pervading control and the sway that one party exercises on the other may be of such degree that is tantamount to encroachment, disqualification and violation of the other person's authentic self.

Let us assume, for the moment, that in our relationship we held that defence that overruns borders and identities, under check. Even if that defence did not play a major role in our life I believe that the relationship with your father left you with such an inordinate resentment that you were bound to settle accounts with me and reproach me for your father's failures. The price I had to pay for having deceived you once was out of proportion with the crime: public scorn, literally a public lynching in the best tradition and loss of employment. Strangely, an inscrutable Christian creed considers that the vanquished not the victors are more often the winners in the eyes of God. But instead, with horror I watched you gradually turning against me and ultimately I became deprived of you, the only woman I ever loved and keep on loving. I don't seem to desire, need or be attracted to any possible replacement. You fill my body, my soul and my destiny by day and by night. You must think I am pretty regressed, masochistic and weak. Is thralldom a weakness of character? Am I pursuing a shadow, a trait, the remnants of something else? Have I come to anchor in the dark continent of my dreams?

If I remember correctly in your remote past you had years of prostration to love which you overcame by a period of sexual acting out. I did act out for a very short period of time with dire consequences.

I rather wait for you even if you promise nothing. If God listens to my prayers you will never regret it: I will be your staunch ally, your idolizer, your fetishist, your right hand, you most dependable, reliable and unfailing partner and, sans arrière-pensée, I swear on my mother's grave, I shall never leave you again. Further, I will respect your need for space and self development.

Our house has been shaken by the winds of disaster which left you bitter with recriminations and suspicion but, as you know it took Ulysses seven years to find his way back home and put things straight. Out of this ordeal you have gained strength and independence, you have held things pretty well together but you have almost forgotten about the role and place a partner and father ought to have at home.

My soul-mate, please, try to treat me like a human being, like the father of your children, like somebody who might one day come to your rescue and who reveres you.

Another of your reproaches is about my relationship with our son. Philippe Julien in an enlightening book (*'Le manteau de Noe. Essai sur la paternité'*: Desclée de Brouwer, Paris 1991) noted than today more than ever in history there is an undermining, a decline, a devaluation, a liability, a constraint and even an imposture impregnated in the father's authority. There are many social and political reasons for this change but among the psychological ones there is an unremitting attack on the father's place and role at home, on his worthwhileness and more insistence and exposure of his flaws and fallibility. As Freud had already pointed out there is no question that parenthood can be 'an impossible profession'.

For Julien, a Lacanian psychoanalyst, it is the mother who registers a place for the Name of the father (*'Le Nom du pere'*) in the symbolic order of the child. The Name of the father becomes in the child's unconscious a phallic signifier or a paternal metaphor which points to what is lacking in the mother - not in terms of an organ or an image - but in terms of a signifier of the mother's desire: *'The real father could be strong or weak, present or absent, gentle or tyrannical, hard working or negligent, faithful or unfaithful to his wife... It doesn't matter...'* (p.40) Julien affirms that there is no real paternal authority except that which the child receives from the woman. What the mother is capable of doing with the father's discourse determines the outcome of that process of introjection of the paternal authority. Based on that beginning the child builds up an image of the father who comes to

73

represent the Law, the threat of castration, the border between the child and the mother as well as many unpalatable prohibitions. Thus the father gradually becomes for the child not only an ideal, a model of identification, but he also a judge, a rival, a threat, a dissembler and a source of ambivalence. These various images are nurtured not only by the father's real behaviour towards the son but by the mother's attributions to that man based on her own, assumed or disowned, image of her own father or other men in her life..

I know that you care about me and you show it in your own ways by acts of cuddling or cryptic messages for which I am grateful and am still savouring every instant of those last marvellous but fleeting times. I also understand why you resisted my advances. Had I stayed longer you would have ended up consenting. By sleeping with me you acted under the presumption that I was not going to force you to have intercourse. You were trusting me for which I am also grateful. We know each other's bodies and soul intimately. It would have been disheartening to make love to me knowing that I was going to vanish again. Besides you did not want to re-open the wound. You have been working hard at overcoming and erasing me of your heart. You had to keep me skin deep and you did a good job at that including using your male friend as a defence and a decoy. After two decades my love for you remains invincible, unconquerable, all powerful... You deserve the best and God tells me I am now prepared to give you that goodness. I want you to know that I am not blaming you for anything. I am just making observations and hating myself for having been responsible for the current state of affairs. It was an unfortunate socio-political chain reaction for which I am spell bound. I often dream that I have not really lost you and that you still love me. For ages you are the only maiden who was allowed to enter my aura, my world of incantation and my centre of gravity. There will be no happiness for me until I am at your side, closing my eyes, resting my head on your bosom and feeling your arms holding me tight. I shall embrace and kiss you ardently and lead you into the spirit of fervour, blushing with tenderness. My silver-footed Queen the music of your voice and your dreamy eyes will heave me into an endless ecstasies. But I know that at first my invocation and invitation to break the barriers would go unheeded. When you recognize the familiar territory and are confident of me and of yourself, you will be able to make a prodigious leap forward and my burning offering will dissipate any bitterness or fear that you might still be harbouring. I have to pull out the knife from my heart, I have to weed out your waverings, I have to pamper and indulge you and you have to remove your masks and to stop setting me up to be somebody I am not. There is not a moment I don't want to be at your side. I have so much to tell you I could write a book.

I love you through the times and through the many former lives.

The Knight of the Sorrowful Countenance
'El Caballero de la Triste Figura'
(Don Quixote)

"A woman would be more charming if one could fall into her arms without falling into her hands (Ambrose Bierce).

To be in love with love is to be a self-seeker, to live for oneself alone, to plunge into dissipation and self-indulgence, to pursuit pleasure, voluptuousness and the sensations evoked by love without much regard for the other.

To see what money can do to influence love or what money can buy to further love is to prostitute love...

To act miserly and rapaciously is to place monetary interest, the reap of profits and filthy lucre ahead of love.

75

True love is loftiness of purpose, magnanimity and self-abnegation.

The question is whether love makes the world go round or Whether money makes the world go round.

There are those cynics who speak of the aristocracy of money; those who say that there is nothing that money cannot buy; those who weight the value of money versus the value of love and those who see money as the sinews of love.

There are the extremes; love madness and money madness.

And those who found no solace neither in money nor in love.

Money is power and a person may seek power and lose freedom; Equally, a person may seek love and lose freedom.

Wanton love and love of power are on the fringe of corruption and vice. As there is hard won money there is also hard won love. Can money buy a person's dignity?

Can true love be reduced to an economic equation?

Economic depression or love lost have resulted not infrequently in suicide. For some people self-worth may represent a monetary sign or the feeling of loveability, Money can also represent food, love, security, worth, status, power and libidinal investment.

Love can represent equally all those characteristics. Often one hears that time is money and that love is timeless. Money can be spent wrecklessly or squandered, which speaks against a timely and orderly sequence in money matters. Love is more often time-bound than timeless.

Money is associated with gold and the gold standard of love is gold but also flowers. While gold lasts flowers wither."

Poems

REQUIEM FOR A MAN

Lifting the veil, I see the relief of your substance
Cascading on my being with luscious indulgence.
Oh, you creature of love, do not open the floodgates of
By-gone times with its torrid memories.
Allow just a drop of dew to fall on the red petals of your
lips;
Allow just a drop of dew to fall on your runaway glance.
There is no place in your essence for me except the
inscription
Of a name, Jacobo, which became the remnant of a dream
Of never-ending love flowing into a sea of uncertainty
And an epitaph that read:
'He had neither prudence nor ballast;
He was a vagabond and a poet not fit for this world
And a renegade with a roving eye;
A man of straw who could easily flounder in the dense fog.
Some said that death surprised him at sea during a fierce
storm
And others said that he died of a broken-heart, alone,
in a run-down plane looking at spider-webs.'

Oh you, bewitching nullity, who timely went under cover
Behind a screen of mystification...
I pursue you relentlessly in your spectral substance
To find nothing but a cipher,
A burst of laughter and jubilant flush.

REQUIEM FOR A WOMAN

The contrasting element of fire and water
Coming to a head in a turning point
Kindling, burning and consuming,
Dewy, wet, dripping and watery;
A hot-blooded demon in a hot bed
Falling under a spell
Which she finds unbearably inflamed.
Teeming mater-familias
Out of joint in the stillness of the silvery lake
Please, do not touch, your hands are burning my body
Just lie still, lull yourself to sleep...
Where are we heading to?
Do not cause any ripples in the quiet surface of my body
The last paroxysm of ecstasy
Came in a dreamless sleep
Boring my soul in an unnameable location
As you were fading away in those voluptuous moments
And became a mere delegate of strangers
Dreaming the dream of other lovers who were
Ravishing me in the moonlight
With the wind blowing on my back and
Swooning me into a trance.

THE LIGHTHOUSE

The splendour of your glow
Dazzled me in its brightness;
I adore your well proportioned breast,
The murmur of your heart,
Your unstinted fountain of pearly tears,
Your shapely legs made of the finest marble,
Your long fingers fondling me in the darkness,
Like fluttering wings of doves,
Your amorous glances and sighing kisses while
The rainbow plays on your black hair and green eyes
Heavenly Beethoven's sonatas.
What has become of the favourable conjunction of stars
that guided us in our dream of eternal love?
Do you find yourself at the end of your tether?
Or are you just teetering at the low ebb of love
Waiting for the mask to fall?
Have we missed the portent of mourning ahead
Predicted by a maiden in black attire?
You, the lighthouse of my life, why have you
Turned your lights dimmer and dimmer for me until,
This lost ship of love, sank
At the shores of your body in an eclipse of meaning.
There were other omens as well such as
A falling and dying star
Succeeded by a blinding snow blizzard
With blustering winds that
Swept me off thy orbit
And threw me, lovelorn, gloomy meek and
Forsaken into a sea of sneering people
Where I, not being able to find a trace
Of your lovable enchanting self which

Once I barely graze as it stung me with its venom,
Drifted endlessly in the wind's eye.
Oh you soul-stirring, tantalizing Queen of the night
Turn on my guiding lights once more and
Allow me to render my last breath
On your splendid bosom
As you rock me into the final departure.

WHERE HAVE YOU GONE?

Bliss is to bask in the gleam of your glance
Heaven is to be at the centre of your being
Now that I have lost you for ever and ever
Now that I am seeking solace in that last
Evanescent memory of a reluctant kiss and that
Your divine essence haunts me in empty places while
I am wandering aimlessly in dark corridors
Looking for that inviting gesture and that
Bewitching smile that had me enthralled.
Now that I have lost you and myself I found a number, a name...
Are you eloping in the sidereal spaces beyond my reach?
Have I left a cue, a mark in your unattainable being?
Have you seen odds and ends of me floating about?
Have you felt any stellar dust
Being blown on your resplendent body?
Which in a twinship of infinite sets I fathom
Million of light years away or
Are you just around a corner slipping by
In the flash of a second in this losing game
Called life?

Am I still falling?
Are you still running?
Who set this whirlwind in motion?
Who abandoned whom?
Are you within?
Are you without?
Are we somewhere?
Are we nowhere?
Are you down there?
Am I elsewhere?
Are you where you are not?
You are not, you are not...

NIGHTMARE

Forgotten, consigned to oblivion,
Foregone, irrecoverable, lost while
I am seized in a spell of frozen silence while
I am entombed in a crypt of quiet turpitude
In a last breathless spasm of languishing yearning
I see my double walking along an endless road of cypresses
Staring in the far distance the sinuous roundness
Of twin mountains which evoked your radiant breasts as
I kisses them fervently earlier times and
Your last embrace had the fragrance of honeysuckles which
Disconcerted me
Because it just occurred before the heroes had fallen
Before the ill-fated last battle where we found ourselves
Crying over corpses and fragments of dreams
And trembling over ominous clouds gathering while
I staggered in the fields struck by a thunderbolt and

In a flash of agony I saw
Your majestic image fading in an instant
Before I was able to reach my destination...
Before I was able to reach my destination...

JEALOUSY

O beware, my Lord, of jealousy,
It is the green-eyed monster which doth mock
The meat it feeds on (Shakespeare's *Othello*).

That man is captive of a restive, grudging, belittling
And tenacious doubt called jealousy believing that
He is an expendable item, that he would be, with no effort,
Replaceable
That he is usurping the place of somebody else and
That he is a double of a double in his lover's heart.
He is living in a world of banishment and torture,
He is living in a world of appearances and substitutions
Looking compulsively at the lurid and shady,
At the hidden, unutterable and indefinable.
Wallowing in hints, half-truths and veiled innuendos,
Living in a world of masks which mock his sense of reality
And urge him to descent into a solitary and loveless world
of
Ghosts where misproportions, defacements and blemishes
are
Rampant.
There are neither flashing revelations nor certainty
Only a gnawing and haunting doubt and an acrimonious
battle.

Who is really the target of your ceaseless cavil and qualm?
Who is betraying whom? Is she really living in a world of
Frivolity or are you creating your own monsters?
Who provides the nutrients for this depleting self-torture?
Who is driving you, senseless Otello, to actualize your worse
Fears?
Where is this cryptic and sneering demon located?: In the
Difference of the sexes, in the identical sex, in the Other,
In the Self, in the essential triangularity of the mind, in
The reflection of a deforming mirror, in the past, in the
Collusion and complicity of two or in the incompleteness
of
The one? Who is the real rival in her affections?
Why did you allow yourself to descent to the horror
Of seeing reality and with it what you love most as
Perishable, impermanent and provisional?
You, precarious creature of a fleeting and killing time
That cannot be put at a standstill
You precarious creature of a doubt that cannot be reversed
You precarious creature of a signifier:
Tolstoy's 'Kreutzer's Sonata' drawing you away from Her...

THE MUSIC OF LOVE

In love you shall find a touch of the divine, a touch of
sorcery,
A touch of madness, a touch of slavery, a touch of grief...
In love we may travel through flirtation, wooing, fondling,
Pastoral tranquillity, labour, dissonance, recurrent sorrows,
Raptures of tenderness and misgivings.
In love we are elevated to scintillating merriment, to the

Sublime and we are let fall to pointlessness, weariness,
Languor and self-loathing.
What is the tune of love? A rhapsody in blue?
A serenade, a fantasia, a rondo, a minuet, a nocturne?
An allegro passionato, an adagio, a lullaby?
Is it a solo within a duet within a trio?
How long does it take for love to become tuneless?
Johannes Brahms never ceased to love Clara Schumann.
"Von ewiger Liebe" op 43... I love her more than myself...

His fourth Symphony in mi minor op.98 is elegiac and
tragic.

Are we bound to be like Orpheus who tamed wild beast by
playing

His cithern and descended into hell in search of Euridice?

Was his end sadly evocative of the fate of love?: He was
torn

Into pieces by the Bacchantes; perhaps his tune failed him
when

He needed it the most.

Woman of my life, woman of my death have you heard
yonder

A violin lamenting?

You have convened a meeting with a man and you
dauntlessly flew

From me with a glee in your eyes.

Broken trust, broken dreams, broken hopes...

The time has come...

The time has come...

A KALEIDOSCOPE

You were diaphanous, transparent and serene until
A turbid stream made you impervious to light.
Was it the harbinger of a transmutation?
Who was responsible for that murky stroke of the brush
On the unblemished canvas of your soul?
How did that sombre transition occurred?
You went through the many tones, the may hues, the many
shades,
  Mellow, vivid, blues, yellows, hazy,
  You were elusive, retiring, fugitive...
From a graceful, stylish, refined tableau you turned into
A shadowy, grey, opaque, livid and discoloured one.
Have I not shielded thee, my precious art form,
From myself and from the ravages of time?
Have I myself become 'Dorian Gray'?

TO RABINDRANATH TAGORE

Truth and falseness,
Meaning and meaninglessness,
Death and immortality.
The cycle of the Seasons,
Nothing ends,
The spiritual fervour,
The spirit of renunciation,
Purity of heart,
Reverence for life,
The sun within,
Search for wholeness,

Flight from the trivial,
Divesting myself of the material,
The principle of harmony and simplicity,
I want to be able to overcome the darkness of desire,
I want to be able to overcome impermanence and to attain
Cosmic consciousness, the Essence, the Light...
I want to be able to throw away masks and envelops,
To be able to free myself from ties,
To be able to transcend appearances...
To be able to regard time and immortality
Internal and external reality, the past and the present as
Tricksters that conceal a more inviolate and unfading
Essence.
I would like to be able to... but I cannot... I cannot...
I should have never departed from thy moorings,
Your conclusive sobbings have taken hold of my heart for
ever.
I'm now crying and sighing in uninhabited dwellings and
Only the memory of your footsteps accompany me.
What senseless, disparate, discontinuous, strange world...
How can I let die the flame you ignited?
How can I let you go, let you die for me?

PERSEPHONE

Has it come the time to open the windows
To the Lady from the world of Shadows?
Rushing in she comes in the dark
And a breeze of a glacial embrace
Seizes upon his fainting heart
Lulling him into a bewitching sleep

Filled with dreams of a dreamless and eternal night,
Dreams of timelessness and mindlessness,
Dreams of no-return and of an uninhabitable absence and
Dreams of not dreaming dreams of desire, vanity and regret.
Alone and unnoticed, the knight, found himself strolling
down a narrow path in forbidden lands,
Leaving without a farewell or a ceremony and
Dying the agony of a deathless soul.
As the knight vanishes in the devouring shadow of the
Lady of the night a glimpse of a struggle is suggested while
The goddess in a frenzy of passion envelops him in her
arms.

EURYDICE

Eurydice... Eurydice... What has become of Orpheus?
We all know that Orpheus is inconsolable and that
He refuses to relinquish you;
What shall you do?
He insists on retrieving you from the world he is not allowed
to enter.
He is threadbare and dried up since you left him
And still bend on destruction he defies the instruction not
to look back
Eurydice who are you really?
What secret rites have you hidden from Orpheus?
Have you become a pagan goddess?
Are you the serpent-goddess in the underworld?
Are you engaged in ritual sacrifices?
Have you gone into the wild of the forest?
Are you worshipping Dionysus?

Who is indulging your thirst for lust?
You thirst for revelry, dancing, drumming and humming?
Who transports you to the heights of ecstasies?
Was Orpheus an intruder into your shocking realm?
On whose orders was he torn to pieces by the Maenads?
On whose orders was he rendered speechless and tuneless
for ever?
First he lost his cithern and with it his musical charm
Then he lost you
And after he was brutally eliminated.
Was he too indomitable in his determination to take you
away
From the life you had chosen?
Did he become a nuisance?
Now in all soberness he cannot rescue you
Now no longer will he be pressing you cause he is dying in
the
Dream-land of
Once upon a time...
Once upon a time...

CHILDREN OF LOVE

Children of my dream
Who heard countless fairy-tales
Who were nursed and rock-a-bye with songs of love
With milk flowing plentifully from
An obliging and large-hearted mother who
Elicited their innocent smiles while
She was transfixed in a glance of desire and
Nurtured sweet dreams of everlasting joy which

Included paterfamilias insinuating himself in-between
With rhymes of transporting love...
But one day that wonderful world was devastated
As the children's tears and clamour wrenched the father's
heart:
'Daddy, don't leave us'
But somebody was insensible to their plight
Somebody is laughing instead of crying
Somebody is looking cunningly elsewhere while
The children kept on spilling tears of pain, tears of hunger,
Tears of fear, tears of loneliness, tears of abandonment...
Tears that knock at the father's door endlessly and kept on
Drilling at his memory unmercifully...
Tears that kept on begging for love lost to return,
Tears that kept on begging for restoring what once was,
Tears that kept on begging for promises to be kept
Tears that shall never cease to be heard
Tears that are a reclamation of restitution of what cannot
be,
Cannot be... a dream of everlasting love in a magical
paradise.

HOME

Home is the recondite, the intimate, the concave,
The innermost recesses of your being;
Home is the fireplace that warms us
And radiates the light of your eyes;
Home is a shelter, a hiding place, a safeguard...
Home is the container, the portmanteau, the cradle...
Home is you...

I can still hear the whispering, soothing, gentle words of
Love that you once copiously shed on me,
I can still remember that never fading sublime moments
with
You,
I wish I could call up the spirits,
I wish I could be at your feet,
I wish I could cast a spell on you and
Find that enchanting word that you couldn't resist,
That enchanting word that would conjure up your soul to
my
Beckoning
And transform instantly a harrowing reality...
But I cannot find that enchanting word anywhere in this
heap
Of debris... I cannot find it...

TO ABELARD AND ELOISE

"Misshapes the beauteous forms of things:
We murder to dissect".
     William Wordsworth's *'The Tables Turned'*

Abelard, revered scholastic philosopher, priest and
theologian,
You a man of bearing and substance...
What crime have you committed
That deserved such an outrageous punishment?
Why has the institution of your forebears,
In an inauspicious moment,
Rendered you an eunuch, tortured you, belittled you and

Banned you from your beloved?
Your soul was fully possessed by a divine light
And by an overwrought Eloise who
In her delight and secret vows
Turned the tables and eloped with you beyond the sunset,
In a decisive act of audacity,
Thrusting into each other's bodies and souls,
In a determined quest for godliness.
In spite of the cruel auto-da-fe we know that your love for
Eloise and her love for you survived and flourished.
Perhaps, you didn't really
Lay down your arms, you, martyr of a love story?
Abelard what crime have you committed
Except to yield to your last and greatest temptation?
Which deprived you of your virility but not of your speech.
Eloise shall keep on writing to you...
Eloise shall keep on writing to you...
Though there shall be no more rejoining...
No more forgathering...no more rejoicing...

SECRET PHANTASM

You opened to me the gates to your mythic, extravagant,
Wanton and preposterous world of ensconced, hushed up
Fantasies where faceless lovers would tie you up,
Judge you harshly and force you to submit to an iron Rule
with no appeal, no mercy.
In your reverie, lovers would avail themselves of your body
As they pleased...
Some lovers were thought to be divine, others were humans
and
Others equine, often turning in their roles male to female
and

Female to male.

Some of them evaporated while others would swarm to you
Eliciting a blush, a quiver, a thrill in your complacent and
Splendid body.

While you were absorbed, panting and pulsating in this fantastic

World of yours I would stray in the woods.

O, delectable Ishtar, Cybele of my dreams, you lay there
Unwillingly naked, exposed and ravished through no fault of

Your own.

You were the victim of cosmic and archetypal forces of vulgar,

Crude, coarse, rude, rough and intimidating cave men and beasts.

You were the victim of the powerful to whom you surrendered

In utter self-denial.

There was no resistance, no malice... you just granted their
Perverse wishes saintly.

Was that an act of uppermost obedience to a higher deity?

Quietly, for fear of disturbing you, I lay there in the dark,
Me, artless scapegoat of the phantasm of others,
I was contented to hover behind your insatiable hinterland
Waiting for the revelry to end and
Loving you more as you came to an earth-shattering orgasm,
Loving you more...

THE TAROT

Who wants to make a bet on the future of a luckless man of
the
Turf who had an aptitude for tempting fortune?
This desperado Dr. Faust can only be redeemed by the
woman
Of his dreams.
Only She can transform hard times, ill-wind and blight into
Sunshine and bliss.
Even her silence will be crowded with whispers of flowers
and
Eternity.
He spent his dog-days under a broiling sun looking for a
fix
In her imaginary body as he was illiterate in matters of the
heart.
He would find joy in watching her dress glamorously and
exquisitely after a steam bath.
At dawn he still waited awake for her return of a night out
With her lover
On day she examined his Tarot cards after the throw of the
dice and thoughtfully her countenance grew sombre.
It doesn't really matter for he is a gnostic, a lost soul on an
alien mission.
She would have no sympathy for his predicament
Nor God would have mercy on his substance.
As he caused too much trouble for everybody
He took to the road as a pariah without parity.
There shall be no miracle. He was sentenced to dwell in a
limbo of love which is ripping his heart.

BANSHEE

Invisible keenings on the fringe of the West Wind,
Singing in the shrouds, I sense your awesome presence,
O, Banshee, Banshee, why have you come?
You have already taken hold of my soul and
Left me for dead, sucked dry in a waste.
But your very nature preys on my mind and
Is weaving dreams in my heart and
Is clouding over my vision.
I cannot escape from thy spell,
I can no longer understand ordinary language
Nor can I sail through the terrifying maelstrom of the sea
Nor can I stop crying for the woes of this world
And yet I am still languishing of love for you.
And each lonely road I take
Lead to an impossible fork where
I find you, ethereal Banshee, dressed in your green,
Flowing robes, inviting me with an enchanting glance
To merge with your haunting spirit.
You know that I have not been responsible for the Babel
tower,
That I have not been responsible for the countless wars
That I have not been responsible for the Holocaust
That I have not been responsible for the dying of the sun
And for the impenetrable darkness that enclosed us
Which incited me to discover my own alien shadow
becoming
A mocking spectre of a fading world
While you were hovering over me
And keeping a tight grip on my fast vanishing life
That had lasted a thousand years pining for you.
Banshee, Banshee would you give me that magical potion?

Would you give me a kiss of deliverance that
Would reprieve me from this karmic cycle and,
At last, would free me from this invincible curse?
That has plundered my life with counterfeit hope,
Would you? Would you...?

POWER

Beware of helmeted battle-ready maids
Beware of those indomitable breastless warriors
Crowding the streets of nameless cities and
Holding the reins of a dreadful carnage and
Feasting, gleefully, over the many spoils of war.
Amazons, Amazons, who is turning the tide of the battle in
Troy?
Who is retreating in disarrayed and leaving
A trail of dying and mutilated bodies?
O, Penthesilea, you were without par among the powerful,
The bravest and the unflinching warriors but
You had to challenge Achilles who
Dispensed you the fatal blow and, to his amazement, when
Tearing off your helmet
Was so overwhelmed by your beauty that, lustfully, did
not
Hesitate to rape your still feverish remains as if he had loved
You for ever and ever while the last defiant surviving
Amazons found their hiding place in their remote
motherland.
O, Amazons, Medea, Moirae, the Erinyes,
And why not, Phaedra and Zuleika who got their revenge
By accusing the object of their love of

The very opposite of what they have committed

And you have come bloodthirsty, avenging, envying and lustful

To demand ritual sacrifice under new guises.

But whoever you are, would you give me back Penthesilea?

For you know that I am not Achilles and

Have not been responsible for her slaying.

You, unconquerable women, with all my battles lost, I knock at your gates imploring you for another chance to try.

Because of a derision of justice and a trick of fate I have

Been disfranchised and sentenced to a life of social death,

Dereliction and vagrancy in an inaccessible corner of the earth

For crimes against humanity attributed to me by the implacable

Furies.

Would you teach me the magic word to enter your world?

Would you let me into your sanctuary?

Would you spare me the ultimate exile?

Would you take me as a slave and your servant

Me, who, unremittingly, would submit to your orders,

Being at your feet,

Bearing your harshness, your contempt,

Your deadly vengeful anger and walking constantly on a tightrope

Bidding for crumbs of your softheartedness

For, I rather embrace your cruelty and pain than your absence.

URVASI

Emerging from the ocean, daughter of pleasure,
I have seen you dancing seductively and
Capriciously in your wanton and lascivious nakedness
That captured me in an orbit of increasing attraction
Which I deemed fatal in a glimpse of dreamy consciousness
For I knew the sea to be treacherous and
I found myself seized by a frantic desire which
Was impelling me utterly to lose my volition
And be caught in irrepressible yearnings
For bits of your favours while, being in suspense
At your mercy, the more you drew away from me the more I
Persevered as I recognize that I owed you my life...
That I owed you my death... that I have erred and succumbed in
The winter of my life and that I still tremble when I am
Approaching you dazzling presence.
I want to see your face, to bathe in your eyes,
To hear the whispers of your invisible worlds,
To hear your sighing and to offer you a timorous rose
As I become imprisoned by the vision of those soft inviting
keen-eyes of yours, your undulating hips, your tempting breasts
And thighs and the swelling waves of pleasure that you
lavished
Upon me.
I woke from this eerie dream thinking that it was you,
In your many disguises, who visited me in an erotic dream to
Quench my ardent desire for that inimitable familiar you...
For you have stolen my heart. Where shall I re-find it?
In the music of the wind?
Love denied... Love denied...

ON THE EDGE

A thorny question: why the rift, the parting,
The fracture in the rock?
The cliffs of Moher stood so high
That fear of being swallowed by the abysm
Gripped me while you were teetering on the edge
Much to the disapproval of an irate passer-by
Who saw you tempting a dance with death
An omen of my fall in a dreary sea
That had set us asunder from that momentous sign
And marked the beginning of a fault registered in my heart.
In dismay I uttered: why have you smiled me so sweetly
On the edge of the cliffs?
I had no white, red or purple shamrocks with me and
It was a toss up, a leap in the dark
That sealed my future and left that
Indelible imprint of that which once had been.
You can see through me, you can see in me
A reflection of yourself, we can see into each other's soul.
I know that at first I brought wretchedness into your life,
Later you brought agony into mine. Are we not yet even?
Had I seen through the many signs of the powers of
darkness,
Had I trusted my ominous dreams, had I listened to your's
Seances of divination and clairvoyance I might have chosen
To jump and seek the boundless avid ocean to soothe my
ails.
Would we meet again in the soaring heaven-kissing misty
Cliffs that had frightened me to death in a vain attempt
To avoid the inexorable leap in time, the compelling
attraction
To hurled myself into space and perhaps to fly... to glide?

AN ANTIQUE DESK

An antique desk stood there, witness of a distant past
That conjured up spectral visitors of bygone days,
And a compilation of family secrets
Which left invisible writings of untold scripts
And lucubrations of many yearnings involving
Three generations which included you, my beloved,
A dream child of missives never read and
A sender on his knees claiming 'ignoramus, ignorabimus'...
O, Tempora, O, Mores
Muted passions were expressed that tottered the noble desk
And prowling the nights were your ancestors,
Intimating their presence with
The creaking wooden desk and a howling in the wind
Alternating with a sepulchral silence and a hollowed hiss
That sent engulfing tides of fears
And brought me back to the horror of history
To the nightmare of love lost
And of incomplete and unfulfilled lives
Endlessly repeating itself in a dynasty
That had come to a standstill but kept
On wooing at the noble antique desk
In a vain attempt to write the definitive
Book of a story that has come to an end,
That has come to an end...
For each of them... for each of them...

OMNIA VINCIT AMOR *(Love conquers all things)*

Nostalgia for the metamorphosis of your body,
Evocation of your roundness,
Henry Moore's vision of five spherical shapes:
Breasts, buttocks and belly, the three bs...
Growing convexity in its fullness
Which shifts the scene into a temple of love, ora pro nobis...
With life quickening and pulsating inside thee
And a smooth surface full of promises and
A virgin spring with scent of lilies and drops of dews
That makes me feel spellbound at that splendour of nature
About to bring forth the fruit of love and life
Which has tied us for ever and ever...
Love, summum bonum, inbedded in three sort of
satisfactions:
Making love, making bread and making babies,
The latter the more permanent and enduring until
Separation breaks the continuity, frightens nature...
Sleepless nights, I'm waiting for thee,
Letter carrier, I'm waiting for thee,
The tumult of the day concealing the phantoms of the night
In every person and every happening, I'm waiting for thee;
Impenetrable beauty, impenetrable silence, I'm waiting for thee
Waiting for the first cry of the baby,
Waiting for the nursling to sleep in the overflowing
Bounteousness of your breasts,
Waiting for the squeaking infant announcing the break of the
Day
And waiting for your glorious smile, the likeness and matrix
of which would accompany me to the end of times...
To the end of times...

LOOKING FOR YOU

I'm still looking for you...
Let no darkness, let no Lethe
Hinder the last solitary road leading to you.
A long interminable journey through the woods
Has delayed me in countless perils,
Swamps, wild beasts, traps, thirst and famine
Has brought me to my knees in a feat of moonshining and
mirage
And years are gone-by but I'm still looking for you
On that very road where I was despoiled and dispossessed
On that very road still heading north with no grudge nor
reproach
Still lost, rambling inconsolable
In a land no man knows
Still looking for you...

FURTIVE

Everything about you is clouded with mystery,
A precious jewel never worn,
An inviolable secrecy, a reserve and an evenness
Shown by your airy steps eluding the sun,
An inviting gesture frozen in time
And a glance of timid self-consciousness that
Left me wondering about the hidden,
Unquiet, contradictory and throbbing desire of yours
Which is insisting upon the bastions of my memory,
Roaring and breaking against the defenceless shores of my
mind

Bringing aromas of lost worlds
And drowning my sorrows
With your ineradicable and intoxicating presence
Already indwelling in that unreal and shadowy space
Where furtive, ephemeral and transient fragments of you
Are swept away by the stormy stream of life.

MIRACLE

A portentous event has seized the traveller
When he is permeated with a light from nowhere
And a calling without a caller
Turning his incandescent body into a source that
Spells other realities beyond time, distance or death.
Surreptitiously he is falling into an abysmal pit and
As the speed of his fall increases
So does the multiplying beautiful images of her
That orchestrate the weightlessness of his body
In a gesture of overflowing love
As he keeps on falling throughout the centuries
Without losing sight of her playing an adagio of
Infinite adoration without a flutter or a ripple.
Without a flutter or a ripple...

Afterthoughts

The cunnings of finding love have been noticed since earliest times. James G. Frazer wrote in this regard: *"the love chase may be considered a form of marriage among the Kirghiz. In this the bride armed with a formidable whip, would mount a horse, and be pursued by all the young men who are pretenders to her hand. She will be given as a prize to the one who catches her, but she had the right, besides urging on her horse to the utmost, to use her whip, often with no mean force, to keep off those lovers who are unwelcome to her, and she will probably favour the one whom she has already chosen in her heart"* (p.156) and in another context: *"Among the South Slavs a girl will dig up the earth from the footprints of the man she loves and put it in a flowerpot. Then she plants in the pot a marigold, a flower that is thought to be fadeless, and as its golden blossom grows and blooms and never fades, so shall her sweetheart's love grow and bloom, and never, never fade. Thus the love-spell acts on the man through the earth he trod on"* (p.44 - both texts in *The Golden Bough - A Study in Magic and Religion* - MacMillan and Co. London, 1959).

The different words associated with love are based on images whose etymologies and various meanings are presented in vol. 1 and 2 of *'The Interpretation of Language'* by Theodore Thass-Thienemann published by Jason Aronson, New York,

1973. In Sanskrit the verb to love is 'to find taste in her' as in the German 'Er findet Geschmack an ihr'. This primary experience of love is therefore equivalent to sniffle around or to enjoy the good taste and to reject the bad one. Another Sanscrit word 'vanas' denotes desire in the sense of libido, voluptas and ecstasis. A metaphor for love is that related to the earth: Demeter had a crush on Iasion and made her love-bed on the furrows of the plowland which was plowed three times. In the Sanskrit 'langala' is to plow and 'langula' is penis. To cultivate the soil, the Greek 'kalli-ergo' (to make beautiful) and to cultivate or to woo a woman became synonymous. A potion may be used for this purpose. The latin 'venum' as the Greek 'pharmakon' denote either a healing medicine, an enchanted potion (Gr.'philtron', Lat.'venes-rom') used to induce a spell or a poison.

Wyn-land is the geographic term for a dionysiac golden age for which the month of May is symbolic. 'Wonne-monat' was considered a month for lust, the time of the rites of spring.

Another metaphor of love is that related to fire. The striking and rubbing of two pieces of wood, a hard and a soft one, until fire ensues, have been associated with sexual relationships since prehistoric times: *"Now let us play... For never did thy beauty so inflame my sense with ardour to enjoy thee"* (*Paradise Lost* 9:1027). The word to match (also 'to strike a match', Spanish, fosforo and French, allumette) means to marry from the old English 'maecca', mate, which is a nominal form of 'macian' or to make. What do the mates make? The making of fire would be the making of love. Wife from the Greek 'damar' is the one who tamed or yoked. The latin is 'conjux' or yoked together from where comes conjugal. In German 'Gatte' means both wife and husband. In contrast the word maiden 'adamatos' is the untamed, unbroken one from where the word 'adamant', inexorable or unbreakable comes. St Paul urged men to leave their parents and love their wives like their own bodies: *"For this cause shall a man leave his father and mother and shall be joined unto his wife, and they shall be one flesh"* (Eph. 5:31-32)... *"So ought men to love their wives as their own bodies. He that loveth his wife loveth himself"* *(Eph.5:28).*

Venus is the goddess of beauty; Veneris, venereal, Veneris dies, venerdi or vendredi (Friday) they all have the same roots. There is a progression from the latin word for woman 'femina' to 'mulier' (Spanish 'mujer' and old French 'moillier') and to wife 'uxorem' or 'uxor'. We still retain the term uxoricide for the man who murders his wife. The respectful word lady, 'domina' or 'seniora' is the counterpart of the word 'Sir' and 'Senior'.

In a fable by Oesop or Esope a weasel is changed into a beautiful young girl which is named a 'domnola' in latin (from 'domina', mistress). The word weasel (Spanish 'comadreja') derives from the latin 'commater' (godmother) but also means to gossip, 'comadrear'. In French the word for weasel is 'belette' from the latin 'bellus', beautiful and 'belo', white and shining. The reputed ferocity of the weasel which is perhaps evocative of malicious gossiping contrasts with words used, 'belette' that are rather flattering. The Greek word ''philia', friendship; 'xenixe', benevolence; 'hetairike' (that became Hetera or Hetaire, a kind of refined and cultured Greek Courtesan, e.g. Aspasia and Frine) stood for mutual attachment and 'erotike', sexual desire expressed different meanings but the most ambivalent and voluptuous form of love derive from Aphrodite (Aphros, foam, sperm) which refers to the dark, cruel, infernal goddess who resembled Ishtar. For the romantics the words 'amare' (to love), 'mare' (sea), 'amer' (torment) and 'âme' (soul) are linked. It can also be discerned the relation between 'amour' and 'amor' or 'la mort' (death);

love becomes 'un souci (care) mordant' (bites); it is a disquieting state, fountain of 'deuil, pleurs, pièges, forfaits and remords'.

Tristan and Iseult is a tragedy of love showing the effects of the love potion 'glisse (sliding) dans leur coeur, prise au même piège (trap) par l'enchanteur (bewitching) Amour': *"Elle le prit dans ses bras et s'etendit a son côte, lui baissant la bouche et la face. Et bien fort le serra contre elle, corps a corps et bouche a bouche, et trepasse en ce même instant ainsi mourut Iseult pour la douleur qu'elle avait de la perte de son ami. Tristan, lui, était mort de son désir. Iseult, de n'avoir pu arriver a temps auprès de lui. Car Tristan mourut de son amour, et la belle Iseult de sa tendresse"* (p.37, Le Roman de Tristan et Iseult - traslated by Pierre Champion-Cluny Publisher, Paris, 1938)

Stendhal that penetrating observer of love wrote an unsurpassable fragment on love lost: *"Son coeur ne comprend pas d'abord tout l'excès de son malheur; il est plus troublé qu'emu. Mais a mesure que la raison revient, il sent la profondeur de son infortune. Tous les plaisir de la vie se trouvent aneantis pour lui, il ne peut sentir que les vives pointes du desespoir qui le déchire. Mais a quoi bon parler de douleur physique? Quelle douleur sentie par le corps seulement est comparable a celle-ci?"* (p.370 - Le Rouge et le Noir - le Livre de Poche, Paris, 1958). Stendhal cites several passages of 'Don Juan' which immerse us in that mystique of love: *"Yet Julia's very coldness still was kind, and tremulously gentle her small hand withdrew itself from his, but left behind, a little pressure, thrilling and so bland and slight, so very slight that so the mind 'twas but a doubt"* (p.70)... *"Then there were sighs, the deeper the suppression and burning blushes, though for no transgression"* (p.51) and *"...But passion most dissembles, yet betrays, even by its darkness; as the blackest sky foretells the heaviest tempest"* (p.67) and citing Schiller describing the pangs of jealousy: *"Moments cruels: et elle me l'avoué. Elle detaille jusqu'aux moindres circonstances. Son oeil si beau fixe sur le mien peint l'amour qu'elle sentit pour un autre"* (p.355).

A story in the Talmud relates how four great masters, in pursuing the way of the mystics: a) one found the 'splendour' and died; b) the other found it and lost his mind; c) the third one went the way of self-indulgence and debauchery; d) only Aquiba went pure and found healing. The search for love resembles that pursuit of the 'splendour' (Zohar), the 'paradise', the 'ultimate' experience which carries with it numerous risks. The demons in the Talmudic tradition were engendered during Friday (Venerdi) night just before the Sabbat. Gershom Scholem (Zur Kabbala und ihrer Symbolik-Suhrkamp Verlag, Frankfurt am Main, 1960) comments on that elusive quality of the Torah, like a beautiful and well proportioned woman who hides in a recondite room of her palace and tantalizes him whom she wants to seduce without being noticed except by the enthralled lover. The 'word' would reveal itself to the lover who would be able to penetrate the secrets of this mysterious and alluring woman only to the extend of his passion for her. Scholem refers to the word 'Pardes' that literally signifies 'Paradise'. Each consonant of the word Pardes point to different paths to enter the Torah: P for 'pesat' or the literal sense; R for 'remez' or the allegorical sense; D for 'derasa' or the hermeneutical sense and S for 'sod' or the mystical sense.

This journey, not dissimilar from the journey through the lands of love, involves the following tasks:

a) an ability to perceive and to discriminate; b) an ability to separate the demoniac and the satanic; c) to be able to reconcile the judgemental and condemnatory side with the merciful and loving side; d) the ability to bring together (coniunctio) the masculine and feminine side (Yang and Ying: the active and the passive); e) the liberation of the shackled or imprisoned side of the self; f) the lifting or overcoming of the limiting forces of 'the other side', the darker side. Thus in the search for true love the path is perilous and the tasks are herculean. As we pointed out Freud distinguished two components in love that could go separate ways: sensuality (Sinnlichkeit) and tenderness (Zaertlichkeit). Indeed, pessimistically and not without an ironic touch, Freud saw love in terms of its exaggerations, idealisations, narcissistic claims, projections, introjections, substitutions and illusions (Denis de Rougemont, Dictionary of the History of Ideas - vol.3. Charles Scribner's and sons, New York, 1973). Rougemont also cited Voltaire who pointed out the equivocal nature of the word love:

"The name love is given boldly to a caprice of a few days' duration; to a sentiment devoid of esteem; to a casual liaison; to the affectations of a 'cicisbeo'; to a frigid habit; to a romantic fantasy; to relish followed by a prompt desrelish; yes people give this name to a thousand chimeras."

Essentially, Rougemont considers three form of love: a) erotic, b) courtly and c) agape, this latter more oblative and charitable as in Luke 10:29-37: *"who is my neighbour? Jesus answers, him for whom you can do something in particular and who expect it from you."* Courtly love, a passion for the dawn of the troubadours, is nurtured by the obstacles put in its way.

Baudelaire went further in his woeful, weary, surfeited erotic vision of love, thriving on spleen and on nostalgia:

"Mais ne suffit-il pas que tu soi l'apparence,
Pour rejouir un coeur qui fuit la verité?
Qu'importe ta bêtise ou ton indifférence?
Masque ou decor, salut, j'adore ta beauté"

"...Et brulé par l'amour du beau,
Je n'aurait pas l'honneur sublime
De donner mon nom a l'abîme
Qui me servirá de tombeau"...
(*Les Fleurs du Mal - Anthologie de la Poesie Francaise -*
Edited by André Gide - Gallimard, 1949).

Romantic love is exclusive in the choice of the object of idealization and desire and tends to foster a preference for unrequited and despairing relationships.

Irving Singer on *The Nature of Love* (Vol.I,II and III, The University of Chicago Press, Chicago - London, 1987) contrasts the romantic pessimism of Goethe, Novalis, Schopenhauer and Wagner with the anitiromantics such as Kierkegaard, Tolstoy and Nietzsche.

At the heart of the romantic wish is a desire to merge with the beloved as expressed by Catherine in Emily Jane Bronte's *'Wuthering Heights'*: *"I am Heathcliffe - He's always, always in my mind - not as a pleasure, anymore than I am always a pleasure to myself - but as my own being."* Romantic lovers are engaged in a search for oneness, for a shared identity.

Falling in love is a frantic search for an ego ideal, an embodiment of perfection (vol.III, p.384). Singer further cites Francesco Alberoni who noted the relation between grief, depression and falling in love: *"The experience originates in an 'extreme' of depression, an inability to find something that has value in everyday life... is the revelation of an affirmative state of being... Between the extremes of falling in love and staying in love there is a state of being in love... an intimate bond which is a form of companionate love"* (p.385-386). Jean Jacques Rousseau *(The Confessions* - Random House - New York, 1945) described his love for Madame d 'Houdetot thus:

"I was intoxicated with love without an object. This intoxication enchanted my eyes; this object became centred in

her. I saw my Julie in Madame d'Houdetot, and soon I saw only Madame d 'Houdetot, but invested with all the perfections with which I had just adorned the idol of my heart. To complete my intoxication, she spoke to me of Saint-Lambert in the language of passionate love. O contagious power of love. When I listened to her, when I found myself near her, I was seized with a delightful shivering, which I have never felt with anyone else. When she spoke, I felt myself overcome by emotion. I imagined that I was interesting myself only in her feelings, when my own were similar. I swallowed in deep draughts the contents of the poisoned cup, of which as yet I only tasted the sweetness. At last, without either of us perceiving it she inspired me with all those feelings for herself which she expressed for her love. Alas, it was very late, it was very hard for me, to be consumed by a passion, as violent as it was unfortunate, for a woman whose heart was full of love for another..." "The vehemence of my passion of itself kept it within bounds. The duty of self-denial had exalted my soul" (Book IX, p.455 - p.459).

Triangularity or triolism has plagued love relationships. It may stimulate the desire by increasing the insecurity, the desire to hold onto the loved one and to triumph over rivals. Jealousy, the self-torture of imagining a rival taking one's place in a woman's heart, may persist long after the final separation:

"It may not always be so; and I say
That if your lips, which I have loved, should touch
Another's, and your dear strong fingers clutch
His heart, as mine in time not far away;
If on another's face your sweet hair lay
In such a silence as I know, or such
Great writhing words as, uttering overmuch,
Stand helplessly before the spirit at bay..." (E.E.
Cummings: *Collected Poems* - Harcourt, Brace and World -

New York, 1966) For Proust, as pointed out by Singer, the beloved never really belong to the lover. The lover *"never captures her soul whatever he may do to the body and generally she deceives him with other men or women as a way of proving to herself that she is not for sale though she takes money from the man... The loved ones in Proust are always what he calls 'êtres de fuite', being of flight. They are loved because they are elusive, pursuing the inaccessible..."* (p.189). Love in the Proustian sense is its own justification regardless of the qualities of the object. Philoctetes, metaphorically, may be regarded as a crucible of love, suffering from an intractable love sickness:

"He was lame, and no one came near him.
He suffered, and there were no neighbours for his sorrow
With whom his cries would find answer,
With whom he could lament the bloody plague that ate
him up.
No one who would gather fallen leaves from the ground
To quiet the raging, bleeding sore,
Running, in the maggot-rotten foot.
Here and there he crawled writhing always -
Suffering like a child without the nurse he loves -
To what source of ease he could find
When the heart devouring suffering gave over" (Vol.II, p.427 in *The Complete Greek Tragedies*, I-IV Edited by David Grene and Richard Lattimore, University of Chicago Press: Chicago 1959) Mallarmé (*Poesies* - vol.V-Editions Barnard and Westwood, London) in his poem Regilla underlines this agony:

"Hanté du souvenir de sa forme
L'Epoux desesperé se lamente et tourmente
La pourpre sans sommeil du lit d'ivoire et d'or.
Il tarde. Il ne vient pas. Et l'âme de l'Amante,

Anxieuse, esperant qu'il vienne, vole encore
Autour du sceptre noir que leve Rhadamanthe".

The apahanisis (fading) of desire contrasts with the sense of aliveness on being able to re-find the ability to love:

"Not easy to state the change you made.
If I'm alive now, then I was dead
Though, like a stone, unbothered by it,
Staying put according to habit,
You didn't just toe me an inch, no -
Nor leave me to set my small bald eye
Skyward again, without hope, of course,
Of apprehending blueness, or stars" (Sylvia Plath: *The New Oxford Book of American Verse* - Edited by Richard Ellmann - Oxford University Press, New York, 1976).

Hoelderlin, another victim of love lost, described it thus:

"But now my house is desolate; they have taken my eyes,
Even I have lost myself when I lost her. Therefore I wander
Around and indeed I must live like the shades, and
For a long time everything else has seemed senseless to me"

"Aber das Haus is oede mir nun, und die haben mein Auge
Mir genommen, auch mich hab'ich verloren mit ihr
Darum irr'ich umher, und wohl, wie die Schatten, so muss ich
Leben, und sinnloss duenkt lange das Uebrige mir" (pp.62-63 Diotima in Hoelderlin's *Major Poetry* - Edited by Richard Unger - Indiana University Press - Bloomington - London, 1975). This lamentation reached its peaks in William Butler Yeats *'The Sorrow of Love'*:

"And bending down beside the glowing bars
Murmur, a little sadly, how love fled,
And paced upon the mountains overhead,

And hid his face amid a crown of stars"...
"...I would spread the cloths under your feet:
But I, being poor, have only my dreams;
I have spread my dreams under your feet:
Tread softly because you tread on my dreams" (W.B.Yeats
in *An Anthology of Modern Verse* - Methuen, London 1931).

This sense of bereavement and desolation was ably captured
in a poem by Robert Frost:
"...Something sinister in the tone
Told me my secret must be known;
Word I was in the house alone
Somehow must have gotten abroad;
Word I was in my life alone,
Word I had no one left but God".

And further in another poem called *'Devotion'* we evoke a
oceanic metaphor of the beloved one with its 'curves' and
countless fragments of memories:
"The heart can think of no devotion
Greater than being shore to the ocean -
Holding the curve in one position,
Counting an endless repetition"... (*The Poetry of Robert
Frost*: Holt, Rinehart and Winston, New York, 1976).

To die as a result of a broken heart or to bring upon oneself
the materialization of one's worse fears was noticed by the
Kierkegaard regarding Antigone and described in a short story
by Merimée which later inspired Georges Bizet to write his
opera *'Carmen'*.

"Antigone is head over heels in love...so she has fallen in
love and the object of her love is not unaware of it. Now, my
Antigone is no ordinary girl, and her dowry likewise is not
ordinary - her pain (p. 162)... *"He knows that he is loved and*
audaciously ventures upon his offensive. Of course, her
reluctance amazes him... What to him is of supreme importance

is to convince her of how deeply he loves her, indeed, that his life is over if he must give up her love. Finally his passion becomes almost unveracious but only more inventive because of this opposition. With every protestation of love, he increases her pain; with every sigh, he plunges the arrow of grief deeper and deeper into her heart... He beseeches her in the name of the love she has for her father... In the same way our Antigone carries her secret in her heart like an arrow that life has continually plunged deeper and deeper without depriving her of her life, for as long as it is in her heart she can live but the instant it is taken out she must die..." (pp.163-164 in *Either/ Or*, part I by Soren Kierkegaard. Edited and translated by Howard V. Hong and Edna H. Hong - Princeton University Press - New Jersey, 1987). In the same book Kierkegaared writes of 'poetizing oneself out of love with a girl' and in his ironic *'The Seducer's Diary'* he was well aware of the narcissistic component of love when he wrote: *"...For you I love and you alone and everything that truly belongs to you, so that if I stop loving you, I would stop loving myself"* (p.404).

In Bizet's Opera *'Carmen'*, a tragic story of jealousy, Don José, a soldier in the Spanish Army, falls in love with Carmen, a wild gypsy girl who is a member of a gang of gypsy smugglers in the mountains. At the camp Don José discovers that Carmen has fallen in love with Escamillo, a brave bullfighter. Insanely jealous Don José wants to kill Escamillo. At that point Carmen has decided to end her romance with Don José. He pleads her to love him but she refuses while noticing the wild look in his eyes. At the height of Escamillo's triumph in the arena, Carmen takes off the ring that Don José had given her earlier and throws it into his face. Don José livid with rage and jealousy stabs her. When he realizes that he has killed the woman he loves he cries out his heart with grief.

Passionate love creates strange bedfellows as La

Rochefoucauld indicated: If we judge love by the majority of its results it rather resembles hatred rather than friendship... The more one is in love the more one is not far from hatred (*"si on juge de l'amour par la plupart de ses effets, il ressemble plus a la haine qu'a l'amitié"; "Plus on aime une maitresse, et plus on est prêt de la hair")* (*Maximes el Reflexions* - Editions Gallimard - Paris, 1965).

Passionate love is indeed a curious hybrid, a state of being that summons up imagination and passion, the flux and reflux of nature, the luminous and twilight intensities of emotions, a repetitive likeness that reminds us of a copying devise though one is usually persuaded of its uniqueness, an almost religious sense of truth and beauty (Pascal's heart reasons) and a situation at risk where the moral imperatives and the categories of logic, causality, time and space are tenuously applicable. Paradoxically a person may realize that he is in love because he suffers all the pangs attributed to being in love (*"...et on ne sent aussi qu'on est amoureux que par sentir toutes les peines de l'amour"* La Rochefoucauld's Maximes).

Antoine de Saint-Exupery, in his poetic simplicity, finds four felicitous words that point to love: taming which more akin to subjugation and domestication; a bond which implies a true love knot; the making of a growing need and a sense of the uniqueness and irreplaceability of that person.

"Qu'est-ce que signifie 'apprivoiser'?

C'est une chose trop oubliee, dit le renard. Ca signifie 'creer des liens...

- Creer des liens?

- Bien sur, dit le renard. Tu n'es encore pour moi qu'un petit garcon tout semblable a cent mille petits garcons. Et je n'ai pas besoin de toi. Et tu ne'as pas besoin de moi non plus.

Je ne suis pour toi qui'un renard semblable a cent mille renards. Mais, si tu m'apprivoises, nous aurons besoin l'un de l'autre. Tu seras pour moi unique au monde. Je serais pour toi unique au monde..." (p.68 - *Le Petit Prince* - Gallimard, Paris 1946).

To be captive, to be imprisoned in love is expressed in the German by the word 'Ergriffenheit' (to be apprehended) which is derived from the root 'greifen' (to seize).

As we already pointed out in every intense love relationship a mournful sorrow is inevitable:

"And then you came with those red mournful lips,
And with you came the whole of the world's tears,
And all the sorrows of her labouring ships,
And all the burden of her myriad years"...

And with the sorrows the unrelenting search for the beloved:

"Though I am old with wandering
Through hollow lands and hilly lands,
I will find out where she has gone,
And kiss her lips and take her hands;
And walk among long dappled grass,
And pluck till time and times are done
The silver apples of the moon,
The golden apples of the sun" (W.B. Yeats in
An Anthology of Modern Verse - Methuen, London, 1931).

That exquisite fragility of love, its withering and natural death was observed by E.E. Cummings in a delicate poem:

"...Love, walk the
Autumn
Love, for the last
Flower in the hair withers:
Thy hair is acold with
Dreams,
Love thou are frail

...Do you know? or maybe did
Something go away
Ever so quietly
When we were not looking" (E.E. Cummings: *Collected Poems* - Harcourt, Brace and World - New York, 1966).

Is there a universal language of love or is it expressed differently in different cultures, among different people depending on their profession, sentiment, linguistic abilities, character and situation? Certainly the poet in each cultures is the spokesman for that refined and imaginative collective mind scintillating with images, symbols and feelings.

There are so many cultural myths that excites the feelings of love, fear, lust and helplessness. Literary works such as *The Hunchback of Notre Dame, Dracula, Orlando, Dr. Jeykll and Mr Hyde, Frankenstein, The Fox and Dangerous Liaisons* are infused with danger, eroticism and compassion for man's fracture of the soul or hidden bestial self. It is interesting that the term vamp or vampire refers to a woman who preys on men unlike Dracula's story which refers to a man as preying on women.

Dido and Aeneas, Anthony and Cleopatra, Adele Hugo, Camille Claudel, Mme Bovary, Margarite Gauthier in *La Dame aux Camelies* and *Anna Karenina* are evocative themes of the tangles of love. The Carthaginian queen Dido was seduced and abandoned by the Trojan Aeneas. She killed herself rather than face public dishonour.

The invincibility of love is portrait in the myth of Isis and Osiris. When the latter was murdered by his jealous brother, Isis began a relentless search for his vanished body. The goddess, finally, located most of Osiris' dismembered body except the penis which was substituted by a piece of shaped gold. Then she proceeded to invent the rites of embalming to reverse the forces of decay and putrefaction.

Paul Verlaine (*Poemes Saturniens* - Gallimard, Paris, 1961)
wrote on that mystique of love, which is vaguely evocative of
the idealized maternal image, in his poem '*Mon Rêve Familier*':

"Je fais souvant ce rêve etrange et penetrant
D'une femme inconnue, et que j'aime, et qui m'aime,
Et qui n'est, chaque fois, ni tout a fait la même
Ni tout a fait une autre, et m'aime et me comprend...
Car elle me comprend, et mon coeur transparent
Pour elle seule, helas cesse d'être un probleme
Pour elle seule, et les moiteurs de mon front blême,
Elle seul les sait refraichir, en pleurant..." (p.43).

And again the holding onto that evanescent Other:

"I will not let thee go.
Ends all our month-long love in this?
Can it be summed up so,
Quit in a single kiss?
I will not let thee go..."

(Robert Bridges in *An Anthology of Modern Verse* -
Methuen, London 1931).

Can love be measured in terms of depth, time or degree?:

"Love - thou art high -
I cannot climb thee -
...Love - thou art deep -
I cannot cross thee -
...Love - thou art veiled -
A few - behold thee -
Smile - and alter - and prattle - and die -
Bliss - were and Oddity - without thee -
Nicknamed by God -
Eternity -" (Emily Dickinson's *Final Harvest* - Poems:
Little, Brown and Co. Boston, Toronto, 1961).

But there is usually a yearning to return to that habitation
and man, the wanderer, like Hansel and Gretel, takes to the

road leaving breadcrumbs in order not to lose his way back even if there is nothing to go back to except to the mother of the nine Muses, Mnemosyne:

"...Ouch, but I'm weary of mist and dark,
And roads where there's never a house or bush,
And tired I am of bog and road
And the crying wind and the lonesome hush.
And I am praying to God on high,
And I am praying Him night and day,
For a little house - a house of my own -
Out of the wind's and the rain's way"

(Padraic Colum in *An Anthology of Modern Verse* - Methuen, London, 1931).

The subjection to masochistic love has been likened to a degrading self-denial, to being caught in an inextricable web of tormenting desire and to a rapturous bliss of unconditional devotion and thralldom. The person may abhor the repetition of the experience which he may deem infernal but he may equally be possessed by a consuming yearning and 'Sehnsucht' to return to that state in spite of its flaunting 'dechirement'. Heine expressed the first and Coleridge the second position:

"...War die Hoelle keine Hoelle
Blieb ich doch ein Junggeselle
Seit ich Proserpine Hab',
Wuensch' ich taeglich
Mich ins Grab" (Heine).

Coleridge's 'Christabel' is a bewitching poem of unfulfilled love, grief and nostalgia:

"...They parted - ne'er to meet again.
But never either found another
To free the hollow heart from paining; -
They stood aloof, the scars remaining,
Like cliffs which had been rent asunder: -

A dreary sea now flows between:
But neither heat, nor frost, nor thunder,
Shall wholly do away, I ween,
The marks of that which once has been".
"Time the devourer of all things" (Tempest edax rerum-
Ovid).

Whether we are frightened, as Pascal was, by the infinite
spaces or whether we are appalled by the transitoriness of all
things, as the poets were, we would like to chisel love in an
everlasting present. The sufferings brought on by love is a
source of inspiration and self-overcoming as Proust noted
(Marcel Proust: *A la Recherche du Temps Perdu*. Texte
presente par Pierre Clarac et André Ferré. 3 vol. Paris,
Gallimard, 1954): *"cet amour amene des desillusions, du
moins agite-t-il de cette facon-la aussi la surface de l'âme,
qui sans cela risquirait de devenir stagnante"... "Les rêves
ne sont pas realisables, nous le savons; nous n'en formerions
peut-être pas sans le desir, et il est utile d'en former pour le
voir echouer et que leur echec instruise"* (vol.III, p.183). Love
is a heroic attempt to transcend the boundaries of the self, to
expose and dismantle one's very nature and to penetrate or to
merge into another dimension, another uncharted territory,
another unknown being... love is a reflection of a reflection of
another being, a projection that searches for the ideal, an
internal vibration... and unattainable other... an unknown place
where I rather be: *"car si on a la sensation d'être toujours
entouré de son âme, ce ne pas comme d'une prison immobile;
plutot on est comme emporté avec elle dans un perpetuel elan
pour la depasser, pour atteindre a l'exterieur, avec un sorte
de decouragement, entendant toujours autour de soi cette
sonorité identique qui n'est pas echo du dehors, mais
retentissement d'une vibration interne. On cherche a retrouver
dans les choses, devenues par la precieuses, le reflet que notre
âme a projeté sur elles; on est decu en constatant qu'elles*

semblent depourvues dans la nature de charme qu'elles devaient, dans notre pensée, au voisinage de certaines idees; parfois on convertit toutes les forces de cette âme en habilité, en splendeur pour agir sur des êtres dont nous sentons bien qu'ils sont situes en dehors de nous et que nous ne les atteindrons jamais. Aussi, si j'imaginais toujours autour de la femme que j'aimais les lieux que je desirais les plus alors, si j'eusse voulu que ce fut elle qui me le fit visiter, qui m'ouvrit l'alles d'un monde inconnu, ce n'etait pas par le hasard d'une simple association de pensée; non, c'est que mes rêves de voyage et d'amour n'etaient que des moments-que je separe artificiellement aujourd'hui comme si je pratiquais des sections a des hauteurs differents d'un jet d'eau irise et en apparence immobile-dans un meme et inflechissable jaillissement de toutes les forces de ma vie" (vol.I, pp.86-87).

It was, of course, Shakespeare in *Sonnets* CXVI who best depicted the essence of love:

"Let me not to the marriage of true minds
Admit impediments. Love is not love
Which alters when it alteration finds,
Or bends with the remover to remove;
Oh no, it is an ever fixed mark
That looks on tempest, and is never shaken;
It is the star to every wandering bark,
Whose worth's unknown, although his height be taken
Love's not Time's fool, though rosy lips and cheeks
Within his bending sickle's compass come;
Love alters not with his brief hours and weeks,
But bears it out even to the edge of doom
If this be error and upon me proved,
In ever writ, nor no man ever loved".

Uplifting images of love: 'a marriage of true minds', 'it admits no impediments', love is no love when it alters or forgets. It weathers any storms and it is impossible to put a price on its worth: *"it bears out even to the edge of doom"*.

This sense of the ever lasting is found in John Keats's *Letters to Fanny Browne*:

"The more I have known you, the more I have loved. In every way even my jealousies have been agonies of love; in the hottest fit I ever had I would have died for you... You are always new. The last of your kisses was ever the sweetest; the last smile the brightest; the last movement the gracefullest".

"...Do understand me, my love, in this: I would never see anything but pleasure in your eyes, love on your lips and happiness in your steps... You say you are afraid I shall think you do not love me - in saying this you make me ache the more to be near you. I kiss your writing over and over in the hope that you have indulged by leaving a trace of your honey. Ever yours, my love." That exquisite sensitivity to the lover's demeanour is expressed in Robert Browning's poem;

"Was it something said,
Something done,
Vexed him? Was it a touch of hand,
Turn of head?
Strange that very way
Love begun;
I as little understand
Love's decay".

Antonio Machado expresses that archetypal love in the following poem:

"Amada, el aura dice
Tu pura veste blanca...
No te veran mis ojos;
Mi corazón te aguarda.

El viento me ha traido
Tu nombre en la mañana;
El eco de tus pasos
Repite la montaña...
No te veran mis ojos;
Mi corazón te aguarda...
Eres la sed o el agua en mi camino?
Dime virgen esquiva y compañera,
Arde en tus ojos un misterio,
Virgen esquiva y compañera,
No sé si es odio o es amor la lumbre
Inagotable de tu aljaba negra,
Conmigo iras mientras projecte sombra
Mi cuerpo y quede a mi sandalia arena"
(*Obras - Laberinto* - Editorial Seneca, Mexico, 1940).
Federico Garcia Lorca with his erotic playfulness delights
us in his poem 'Preciosa y el aire':
"Su luna de pergamino
Preciosa tocando viene
Por un anfibio sendero
De cristales y laureles.
...Su luna de pergamino
Preciosa tocando viene.
Al verla se ha levantado
El viento que nunca duerme.
San Cristobalon desnudo,
Lleno de lenguas celestes,
Mira la niña tocando
Una dulce gaita ausente.
- Niña deje que levante
Tu vestido para verte.
Abre en mis dedos antiguos
La rosa azul de tu vientre.
...Y mientras cuenta, llorando,

Su aventura a aquella gente,
En las tejas de pizarra
El viento furioso, muerde" (*Romancero Gitano* - Editorial
Losada - Buenos Aires, 1942).

What Jones calls tha aphanisis of desire is expressed in one
of Garcia Lorca's poems:

"Y despues
Los laberintos
Que crea el tiempo
Se desvanecen
(Solo queda el desierto).
El corazón,
Fuente del deseo
Se desvanece
Solo queda el deseo).
La ilusion de la aurora
Y los besos,
Se desvanecen
Solo queda el desierto
Un ondulado desierto".

After all love spent, illusion dashed and kisses forgotten
only remains an undulating desert. The poet describes an ever
growing conflict between love and disillusionment. As George
Moore points out love is an ideal - something not quite
understood: transparencies, colour, light, a sense of the ideal
hence is bound to experience a rude awakening with time.

Epilogue

This is the narrative of a stormy love relationship between Moira and Vincent. During the course of the many years it lasted several events (intra- and inter-personal) contributed to the wear and tear of their bond. Jealousy, threats of abandonment, emotional withdrawal, unfaithfulness, financial loss, loss of status and other catastrophic events took a staggering toll in their sense of intimacy and togetherness. The many stages that the relationship went through were described in vivid letters and elaborated in a theoretical frame.

Attractiveness, infatuation, offering, merging vs. separation, unresolved conflicts surrounding trust vs. mistrast, dependence vs. independence, love vs. aggretion, dominance vs. submission, conflicting identities were replaced by a sense of privation, disappointment, loss and paralysing grief in the face of adversity. When everything seemed lost the lovers relived every experience from the very beginning. Moira was not able to withstand the shattering events and withdrew her love while Vincent, utterly enthalled, kept on writing her wooing letters which were not reciprocated.

Have men's fantasies about women changed over time or, while maintaining the same basic themes, they have only been shaped according to historical and socio-psychological reality? It appears that each Zeitgeist have their own emerging view of women but that universal prototypes have remained unchanged. Women like Eva, Circe, the Amazones, Medea, the Madonna type, Juliet, Lady MacBeth, Phedre, Isseult, the Geisha and the Hetaire to name just a few prototypes, even if they were, partly fictional products of men's projections, do exist. The play *'Judith'* by Friedrich Hebbel based on the Biblical script and the pictorial representation of her by Horace Vernet is an example of the reputed cunning of a woman to exact her vengeance against Holofernes. Another admirable prototype of forbidden love that survive 'in absentia' against all odds was that of Abelard and Eloise. Abelard died in 1142. Twenty years later Eloise died. When she was buried in the same tomb it was said that Abelard's remains revived, moved closer to Eloise and embraced her.

Pitfalls in comunication, betrayals, lies, disillusionment, separations, love lost and broken promises have often eroded love relationships and have transformed the angelic image of the Other into its very opposite. But who is able to keep promises and illusions nurtered in the heat of passion? In *Loves Labours's Lost*, Shakespeare addresses this point:

> *"Then fools you were these women to forswear;*
> *O, keeping what is sworn, you will prove fools.*
> *For wisdom's sake, a word that all men love ;*
> *Or for love's sake, a word that loves all men;*
> *Or for men's sake, the authors of these women;*
> *Or women's sake, by whom we men are men;*
> *Lets us once lose our oaths, to find ourselves,*
> *Or else we love ourselves to keep our oaths..."* (p.102)

The fading of the subject and its affirmation (metaphorically speaking: master-slave bonds) are at the core of this conflict which in turned is fueled by that elusive and boundless object of desire that charms and frightens the lover: *"lets us once lose our oath to find ourselves or else we lose ourselves to keep our oaths"* (freedom or bondage). Shakespeare sense this awesome truth in *Troilus and Cressida*:

"This is the monstrocity in love, lady, -that the will is infinite, and the execution confined; that the desire is boundless, and the act a slave to limit...

They say, all lovers swear more performance than they are able, and yet reserve an ability, that they never perform; vowing more than the perfection of ten, and discharging less than the tenth part of one. They that have the voice of lions and the act of hare, are they not monsters?" (p.440).

This impossble situation of conflict is also depicted in Sonnet 147:

"My love is as a fever, longing still
For that which longer nurseth the disease;
Feeding on that which doth preserve the ill,
The uncertain sickly appetite to please.
My reason, the physician to my love,
Angry that his prescriptions are not kept,
Hath left me, and I desperate now approve,
Desire is death, which physic did except,
Past cure I am, now reason is past care,
And frantic mad with evermore unrest;
My thoughts and my discourse as madmen's are,
At random from the truth vainly express'd;
For I have sworn thee fair, and thought thee bright,
Who art as black as hell, as dark as night" (p.731).

Thus the parting and the fall seem inevitable as expressed in *Troilus and Cressida*:

"And not a man, for being simply man,
Hat any honour; but honour for those honours

127

That are without him, as place, riches, and favour,
prizes of accident as oft as merit;
Which when they fall, as being slippery standers,
The love that lean'd on them as slippery too,
Do one pluck down another, and together
Die in the fall..." (p.442).

In her *Anthology of Letters of Love*, Antonia Frazer points to several invariants or archetypical images of men's views of women and in the expression of love. John Keats' love letters abounds in these subtleties of the language of love. there is an unpredictability about the fate of desire which René Girard as follows:

"Pour qu'un vaniteux désire un object il suffit de le convaincre que cet object est déja désiré par un tiers auquel s'attache un certain prestige. Le médiateur est ici un rival que la vanité a d'abord suscité, qu'elle a, pour ainsi dire, appelé a son existence de rival, avant d'en exiger la défaite ... Dans la plupart des désirs stendhaliens, le médiateur désire lui-même l'object, ou pourrait le désirer: c'est même ce désir, réel ou présumé, qui rend cet object infiniment désirable aux yeux du sujet. La médiation engendre un second désir parfaitement identique a celui du médiateur. C'est dire que l'on a toujours jouer son role de modele sans jouer également, ou paraitre jouer, le role d'un obstacle..." (p.20-21).

The wooing of the spurned lover knows no limits even when expressed in poetical licence as in this poem of Eluard:
"Elle se refuse toujour a comprendre, a entendre
Elle rit pour cacher sa terreur d'elle même
Elle a toujour marché sous les arches des nuits
Elle a laissé
L'impreintre des choses brisées" (p.84).

The other, the mediator. The ubiquitous mirroring and Mimesis, difference and sameness, the evocation of transference and substitution, the making of a triangularity, the pangs of jealousy, the sense of the unattainability of the object of desire and the value invested are unfailing components of most love relationships.

The Works of Shakespeare - Frederick Warnw and Co. London.

Fraser A. *Love Letters-An Anthology* - Penguin Books - Harmondsworth, Middlesex, England, 1976.

Girard R. *Mensonge romantique et vérité romanesque* - Editions Bernard Grasset, Paris 1961.

Eluard P. *Capitale de la Douleur* - Gallimard, Paris 1966.

Postscript

"...I shall be telling this with a sigh
Somewhere ages and ages hence:
Two roads diverged in a wood, and I -
I took the one less travelled by,
And that has made all the difference"
                    (*The poetry of Robert Frost*: Holt, Rinehart
                                    and Winston, New York, 1976).

There can be little doubt that Neruda was the most significant 'poet of love' of the twentieth century and that he was able to render the most musical and lively poems of this incomparable state:

"Mujer, yo hubiera sido tu hijo, por beberte
La leche de los senos como de un manantial,
Por mirarte y sentirte a mi lado y tenerte
En la risa de oro y la voz de cristal.
...Como sabria amarte, mujer, como sabria
Amarte, amarte como nadie supo jamas
Morir y todavia
Amarte mas
Y todavia
Amarte mas
Y mas..."

"Cuerpo de mujer, blancas colinas, muslos blancos,
Te pareces al mundo en tu actitud de entrega.
Mi cuerpo de labriego salvaje te socava
Y hace salter el hijo del fondo de la tierra.
...Ah los vasos del pecho - Ah los ojos de ausencia -
Ah las rosas del pubis; Ah tu voz lenta y triste...
Cuerpo de mujer mia, persistire en tu gracia
Mi sed, mi ansia sin limite, mi camino indeciso
Oscuros cauces donde la sed eterna sigue
Y la fatiga sigue, y el dolor infinito".

And the contrasting elements of love between being and not being, having and not having, giving and withholding is expressed thus:

"Antes de amarte, amor, nada era mio;
Vacile por las calles y las cosa;
Nada contaba ni tenia nombre;
El mundo era del aire que esperaba.
...Todo estaba vacio, muerto y mudo,
Caido, abandonado y decaido,
Todo era inalienablemente ajeno,
Todo era de los otros y de nadie,
Hasta que tu belleza y tu pobreza
Llenaron el otoño de regalos"
(Pablo Neruda - *Obras Completas* - Tercera
Edicion - Editorial Losada, Buenos Aires, 1967).

Courting with madness, counting the losses, trembling at the day of judgement and drifting alone in bewilderment as a result of the pangs of love are also evoked, better than thousand words by three great poets:

"Lovers and madmen have such seething brains,
Such shaping fantasies, that apprehend
More than cool reason ever comprehends.
The lunatic, the lover, and the poet
Are of imagination all compact:-
One sees more devils than vast hell can hold,-
That is the mad man; the lover, all is frantic,
Sees Helen's beauty in a brow of Egypt..."
                    (Shakespeare's *'A Midsummer Night's Dream'*).

And T.S. Eliot sense that we are 'a straw man' at the core being judged and labelled without appeal:

"...And I have known the eyes already, known them all -
The eyes that fix you in a formulated, sprawling on a pain,
When I am pinned and wriggling on the wall,
The how should I begin
To spit out all the butt-ends of my days and ways?
And how should I presume?"
    (The Love Song of J. Alfred Prufrock in *'Seven Centuries of Verse'* - selected by A.J.M. Smith - Charles Scribner's Sons, New York, 1957).

And finally Ezra Pound in an ambiguous poem called epilogue asked: *'Qu'est ce qu'ils savent de l'amour?*

"For three years, diabolus in the scale,
He drank Ambrosia,
All passes, Ananke prevails,
Came end, at last, to that Aracadia.
He had moved amid her phantasmagoria,
amid her galaxies,
Nuktis' agalma.

...Drifted...drifted precipitate,
Asking time to be rid of...
of this bewilderment; to designate
His new found Orchid..."
(in *The New Oxford Book of American Verse* -
Edited by Richard Ellmann - Oxford University Press,
New York, 1976).

I would like to conclude in a more exulting note;

Patricia Monaghan in her fine study: *'The Book of Goddesses and Heroines'* (Llewellyn Publications - St. Paul, Minnesota, 1990) describes the lovely and haunting Greek legend of Baucis and Philemon who loved each other for so long *"that they became inseparable, almost indistinquishable. Although age bent their backs, their eyes still shone with care and concern for each other; often they told themselves how empty life would be without such love... The gods in recognition of the old couples's kindness, granted them a single wish. The pair wished quickly: to live together forever and never to be separated. Their hut instantly changed into a temple, where they served the gods for years. Then one day, as they stood outdoors, their feet took root and their arms stretched up to the sky, and they lived on forever as a pair of intertwined linden trees"* (pp.281-282).